I0536957

Halls of Light

The Mageborn Saga, Volume 3

Dayne Edmondson

Published by Dark Star Publishing, 2019.

HALLS OF LIGHT

First edition. May 30, 2019.

Copyright © 2019 Dayne Edmondson.

ISBN: 978-0998426372

Written by Dayne Edmondson.

Also by Dayne Edmondson

The Dark Tide Trilogy
Emergence
Eclipse
Ruin

The Mageborn Saga
Mageborn
The Cursed Tower
Halls of Light

The Seven Stars Universe
Ghost Ranger
Space Commando

The Shadow Trilogy
Blood and Shadows
Time of Shadows
Shadows Fall

Standalone
The Complete Dark Tide Trilogy
The Complete Shadow Trilogy

Watch for more at https://www.darkstarpublishing.com.

Table of Contents

Prologue

Zerrecia knelt. Before him, the darkness coalesced into a face, hidden by a hood. "Master."

His master, Valdorf, glared down at him in silence for several long moments, only his red eyes visible in the darkness. Zerrecia did not squirm, however. He knew any sign of impatience or weakness could spell his end. Many a servant of the dark lord had died from such weakness.

"You failed." It was not a question. He might as well have been saying the sun had risen that morning. Not that it had been a foregone conclusion like the sun rising, but it was an observation, nothing more. That chilled Zerrecia more than if Valdorf had yelled.

Resisting the urge to swallow to steel his nerves, Zerrecia retained eye contact and spoke in a calm, measured tone. "Yes, master. Our plan failed."

"Your plan," Valdorf corrected. "You insisted in designing the plan and the failure is upon your shoulders."

"Of course," Zerrecia replied smoothly. "I meant no offense."

"Do not grovel," Valdorf snapped.

Zerrecia did not reply to the command. Such supplication could be taken as groveling. Instead, he continued. "There are other opportunities, my master. Other plans in motion that may yet prove fruitful."

"You assume I will let you live long enough to see those plans bear fruit. We lost the element of surprise with your ill-guided attack." He made no mention of the lives of the cultists they'd also lost. Zerrecia had long ago learned his master did not value human life. And truly, he didn't blame him. Humans were frail, weak things, existing for a fleeting moment in the face of eternity. Their god, though, the true god,

1

Rae'Shela, was eternal. He would show them the way, if they only did his bidding.

Zerrecia did not protest. He did not look away. He did not twitch. "I live to serve and await my death if that is your will." Truth be told, he was not afraid to die. He knew his god awaited him beyond the veil. He hoped his confidence showed on his face.

It must have, for his master did not strike him down where he stood. There in the shadow chamber the barrier between the real world and the shadow realm was thin, almost non-existent. His master could reach out, with his mind if not with his hands, and snuff the life out of Zerrecia in any number of ways. "The *children* who stopped you," he said the word "children" with a sneer, "who are they?"

"I do not know for sure, master. Four of them we encountered in the woods when they were on their way to the Tower. They were in the company of an arch mage of the Tower."

"Yes, the two who held the Staff of Agamar. Who destroyed it?" Another failure of Zerrecia's.

"The very same, master. There was also the daughter of two Eternals there. Isabelle."

"Yes," he hissed. "I met the child in the shadow realm. If not for her mother I would have been free right now." He paused, as if musing some deep thought. Then his eyes re-focused and he jabbed a finger at Zerrecia. "Your new plans will take these children into account?"

"They will, Master. We will neutralize the threat they pose to our plans; I assure you."

"Do not give me assurances," Valdorf said in a low, deadly voice. "Give me results. Fail me again, and you will find yourself being re-placed."

"I will not fail you."

"Go forth and let chaos reign." The shadowy image of his master faded to mist and then to nothingness. Only then did Zerrecia allow himself to take a deep sigh. He looked around to make sure that none of his underlings saw his moment of weakness, but none had dared follow him into the shadow chamber, likely for fear that Valdorf would take his wrath out on them as well as Zerrecia.

"I will not fail," he repeated to the nothingness before him. Whether he was talking to Rae'Shela or himself, he didn't know.

Chapter 1

"How did you do?" Kylie asked.

Emma swiped at the sweat slicking her brow before looking at her friend and shrugging. "I think I did okay. I might have confused the First and Second Selucian Wars, but hopefully he won't mark me down too much for that."

"And you killed it in offensive and defensive magic," Ethan chimed in. "Who cares about history?"

"Those who don't learn from history are doomed to repeat it," Emma said, quoting a phrase their mother used to say.

Ethan shrugged. "Does it really matter who died in what war?"

"It matters why the wars started," Emma pointed out. "Because then future generations," she gestured to herself and the other four people occupying her table, "can learn from the mistakes of the past and not fight pointless wars."

Isabelle snorted. "You really think we can stop war?"

"I said pointless wars. I think we could stop pointless wars where one party is offended at another party and start calling their banners before their cheeks have returned to their normal color."

"Farmers don't start wars," Richard pointed out. "Nobles could learn a few things from farmers."

"Yeah, like how to work with their hands," Ethan said.

"What do you know about working with your hands?" Emma asked her brother sharply.

"Mom was a blacksmith," he said, as if it should have been obvious.

"And you worked with your hands in her shop?" She knew the answer.

"Well, no, but I know the concept."

"Sounds like it's not just nobles that could learn from farmers," Richard jibed.

"Well, I have all summer to learn from you, oh wise master," he said, half-bowing in his seat.

Emma pressed her lips together, fighting back another angry comment about her brother leaving her. *It's just for the summer*, she reminded herself. And they had invited her too. But visiting a farm wasn't her idea of a fun summer break.

"Try being a sailor," Isabelle said. "Ship bucking beneath you in rough waters while you're trying to hoist the rigging and stay on the damn ship."

"No thanks," Ethan said, holding his hands up. "One adventure at a time."

It was Emma's turn to snort. "As if the last year has been anything but one adventure at a time."

"The last six months have been quiet," Kylie pointed out.

"True," Emma conceded. In the wake of the devastating attack on the Tower things had returned to some semblance of normal, with students resuming class and repairs being affected in short order. She sighed at the memory of their experiences. In less than a year they'd learned they had magic, been all but exiled from their home town due to bigotry and kidnapped on the journey to the place they would be trained in using magic. Then they'd become involved in a plot involving insurrection within the Tower itself and barely managed to stop it before more lives were lost. Not exactly an uninteresting life, to be sure, but not one Emma was keen to continue living. She liked peace and quiet. "Are you still going on the ship, Isabelle?" Time to change the subject.

Isabelle nodded. "Yes. My mother wants to continue my shadow walking training. She says I have a lot to learn and a lot to get caught up on and little time."

"Little time until what?" Ethan asked.

Isabelle shrugged. "Maybe she knows something that she's not telling me."

"An assassin being secretive? Unbelievable," Ethan proclaimed in mock shock.

"Former assassin," Isabelle corrected for what Emma knew was probably the thousandth time since arriving in Tar Ebon. Yes, her mother was not technically an assassin any longer, but she was still the deadliest woman, the deadliest person, Emma had ever seen. At least in martial combat. When it came to magic, Alivia was quite formidable and might have the shadow walker beat in a straight fight. *Until Bridgette appears behind Alivia and slits her throat.*

"What about you?" Emma asked Kylie. "Are you staying in Tar Ebon?"

Kylie looked down for a moment and her cheeks flushed. "Yes. Caleb and I broke up."

"Pfft, that guy was a jerk anyway," Ethan said, waving away the boy as if swatting away a fly. "You can do way better."

Like you? Emma wondered. Ethan hadn't shown much interest in the coven refugee over the past school year but, then again, they'd faced death twice and that tended to bond people. The thought of her brother and one of her best friends courting made Emma want to alternate laughing and crying. "Plenty of other fish in the sea," she offered in way of support for her friend. It was a phrase her mother had used when Emma and her own first crush, Dale, stopped being friends at thirteen. Emma had been devastated at the time.

"Besides, you want to finish your schooling before you settle down, don't you?" Richard asked. He was one to talk, with the way he and Melissa went at each other in shadowed corners when they thought others weren't looking. She was even going on the trip to his family's farm with him and Ethan. She'd have been there at their table if not for her defensive magic exam. *Maybe his definition of settling down and mine are different.*

Kylie shrugged again. "I don't know. I did okay in my classes, but my marks weren't great. My adviser suggested I take maybe one more year and decide on a profession outside the Tower."

Emma winced, then tried to smooth her face and coughed to hide her expression. Being "advised" to take a profession outside the Tower, outside of the magical community, was like saying you would be a poor mage and would never make it in the world. It wasn't exactly rude, especially since advisers were supposed to tell their charges the hard truths, but it could be embarrassing for the student. "Well, you like herbalism anyway," she began, "you could go to any village in the Federation and be the best medicine woman in the town."

"And settle down and marry a blacksmith or farmer or something," Richard put in.

Isabelle rolled her eyes but, in a surprising show of restraint, did not speak. Emma had no doubt it would have been something sarcastic.

Kylie sighed. "You're right." Still, the energy from earlier was gone, replaced with something else. Perhaps resignation?

"What about you, Emma?" Ethan asked. "You and your *boyfriend*."

Emma rolled her eyes. She'd been expecting the jab. "Frederik and I are just friends." It was mostly true. They hadn't gone beyond kissing a little, and far less than Melissa and Richard.

"Is he going to stay in Tar Ebon with you?"

"No. He's going back to his family's estate."

"And didn't invite her," Isabelle chimed in. There came the jab, late but never absent.

"We barely know each other," Emma protested. "And he's of a much higher station than I am."

"I don't understand why station matters so much," her brother pressed. "So what if you want to marry the son of a duke or count or whatever?"

"It's about what each marrying party's family brings to the equation, though," Kylie pointed out as if living in a sheltered coven for most of her life had given her some great insight into the workings of Tar Ebon's elite ruling class. Perhaps she had paid more attention in political classes than Emma had.

"Our mother is a famous blacksmith of world renown. That's not good enough?" He sounded hurt.

"It's all right," Emma said, wanting to put the issue to bed for the day. "I don't think I would like it in the south anyways. Way too hot."

"So instead you'll just sit in the Tower and study all summer long?"

"Studying is important," Emma pointed out. She didn't intend for *her* adviser to tell her to choose a profession outside of the Tower. She dreamed of being a professor one day. She would never tell her friends that, though, unless she wanted to be made fun of.

"So is having a break. That's why they call it summer *break*."

"It's more of a break for the professors," Richard commented. "I swear at least one professor wanted to murder the entire class by the end of the year."

"And professors I didn't even have wanted to murder me," Ethan said, puffing his chest up with pride.

Emma shook her head, wryly amused. Indeed, her brother's reputation had spread throughout the Tower. So much that almost every professor they passed eyed him with suspicion, as if expecting a practical joke to emerge from his hands at any moment. How he still managed to prank the other students boggled her mind.

"I'm more of a home body anyway," Emma went on. *Or so I keep telling myself to avoid thinking about why Frederik didn't invite me to go to his estate with him. Maybe he didn't want to make me uncomfortable.* The truth of the matter was she liked him but didn't know yet if she *loved* him. Would their romance retain its heat through the summer months, or would it cool by autumn? *Do I really want to know the answer? What are the odds we'll stay together?*

Would you care for me to provide you with an educated guess of your odds of remaining in a relationship after three months apart? I can fac-

tor in hormone levels, distance, percentage of time absent, experiences with additional attractive members of the opposite sex and seventeen other variables.

Emma shook her head wordlessly at her NIA's offer of help. *No, Shadow, I don't need that. It either will survive or it won't. Knowing the odds won't change things.*

On the contrary, m'lady, knowing the odds...

No, Shadow. Not now. She feared if the neurological interface assistant implanted in her head kept speaking to her she would start to cry. Even now tears were brimming in her eyes and she blinked quickly.

If anyone noticed her silent conversation, they made no mention of it. Her brother and Isabelle also possessed implants, while Richard and Kylie did not. Those two knew about the implants in an abstract way - Emma had told them after the attack on the Tower - but they didn't truly understand it. How could they fully understand an entity inside their head thinking thoughts different than their own, in a strange way no human would?

"I have to go," she said, before anyone else could speak. "Alivia wants to speak with me."

"What does she want?" Kylie asked. Was the girl jealous?

"She didn't say. She just asked me to be to her office by one." She rose. Tomorrow was the day. "Safe travels, Richard and Ethan. Give my best to Melissa. Isabelle, don't die," she smiled at her wit. "And Kylie, you're welcome to join me in the library any time."

"Likewise, you're welcome to join me on the city streets," she retorted.

"Oooh, you can be cutthroats together," Ethan cut in.

Kylie glared daggers at Ethan, evaporating any belief in Emma's mind of the two ever getting together. "I want an herbalist apprenticeship over the summer. Emma could come with me."

Emma resisted the urge to scrunch her nose up at the idea of pummeling herbs to make potions or brews or whatnot. She just smiled as she turned to leave.

"What, no hug for your brother?"

Emma half-turned, then smacked her butt. "You know how to reach me if you want to say hi. I don't think I'll ever be rid of you."

He affected a wounded stance, one hand over his heart. "You wound me."

Emma snorted and left the room. She didn't know what Alivia wanted, the day before school let out for the summer, but she hoped it wasn't bad.

Chapter 2

Emma opened the door to Alivia's office, revealing the arch mage seated behind her desk, studying multiple sheets of parchment, while a black and white map lay unfurled before her. She looked up and smiled at seeing her. "Emma, come in, come in." She beckoned with one of the sheets she'd been reviewing.

"You asked to see me?" Emma asked, nervously. She had seen little of the arch mage during the school year following the attack. She had told her at the time that she was preparing to ensure this never happened again, but Emma wasn't sure what that entailed.

"Yes." She steeped her hands and studied Emma over her fingers. "I have a question for you. There is going to be a parade tomorrow, in the city, and a ball tomorrow evening. I know it is short notice, but I wondered if you would like to accompany me."

Emma blinked in surprise, thoughts racing. "Can Kylie come?" Her first thought was for her friend, who would be left out otherwise. "She's remaining in the Tower for the summer and doesn't have anywhere to go."

Alivia smiled wide. "Of course she can join us. I apologize for not thinking of her sooner. My mind has been elsewhere, and alas this parade and ball crept up on me, as much as I hate to admit it."

"You know the queen, don't you?" Emma asked. She remembered that detail from the stories.

"Yes, we are good friends. Being trapped in a city under siege will do that."

"It must have been scary, fighting the Krai'kesh."

Alivia stared at the wall behind Emma, eyes taking on a distant expression as the memories surfaced. "In hindsight I suppose it was frightening, but it wasn't in the moment. I knew I had to be brave or I would die. There wasn't time for fear to enter the equation. And the queen, well, she had to take control of the situation for the same reason. I was unconscious for part of it, but during the final battle the queen rallied all the townsfolk, all the defenders of the city, to charge out through the gates in a final push. It was a sight to see, the final fight for survival. The way the people put their differences aside and fought a common enemy. I haven't seen that scale of cooperation in any time since then."

"Will we meet the queen tomorrow?"

"Of course. We will meet her at the ball tomorrow evening. I've told her much about your achievements and she is eager to meet you."

"Me?" Emma felt surprise at that revelation. *The surprises just keep coming today.*

"Two heroes of the Federation," Alivia pointed out. "Why wouldn't she want to meet you?"

Emma shrugged. *Maybe because my own boyfriend is embarrassed for me to meet his family.* "I am just a humble commoner. It's hard to imagine a queen wanting to meet me."

"With most queens that would probably be true. With the Empire you would be filled with arrows before you came within one hundred paces of the emperor, but our queen is different. She learned firsthand the value of a 'common' life when the Eternals came. They proved that birth meant nothing, a fact that did not set well with the aristocracy across the continent."

"They obviously overcame it. Or at least Jason and Bridgette and Dawyn did." She didn't know what had become of John and Ashley. The stories didn't say, and even the histories about them in the library of the Tower ended about eighteen years earlier. She didn't think they'd died, for there would have been a state funeral and *that* would have been recorded in the histories for sure. "What ever happened to John and Ashley?" Alivia had trained them, had been friends with them. If she didn't know, no one would.

Alivia smiled a sly smile. "That, my dear is a secret. They are alive, but I can't tell you where they are."

"But the other three aren't in hiding."

"No, they're not. But that was their choice. Bridgette could hardly run a network of spies anonymously. Or at least it wouldn't have been as effective. Her name...well...it opens doors."

"And strikes fear into the heart of her enemies," Emma chimed in wryly.

"That too. And Dawyn, well, he is the supreme commander of the Tar Ebon military. He could hardly command in secret."

"I suppose not," Emma said, curiosity over the identity of John and Ashley still boiling up inside her. But she knew she would get nothing further out of the arch mage than what she'd given her. Well, maybe one thing. "Do you think they'll return one day?" She tried to keep her voice as innocuous as possible.

Alivia shrugged. "I hope so. We could certainly use them in the fight with the Cult of Rae."

Curiosity over a new topic arose in her. "How is the fight against the Cult going?"

Alivia sighed, suddenly looking her age, creases above her eyes spring into focus and her shoulders slumping. "Not as well we had hoped. They've proved more elusive than expected, to be honest. It's as if they went underground and disappeared."

"Or are lurking, waiting to strike," Emma posited.

"More than likely that is the truth," Alivia conceded. "Still. I expected questioning the captives would have yielded more intelligence. Bridgette herself has been practically threatening her network of spies at knife point for information but no one knows anything."

"Sounds frustrating."

"You have no idea. We are vulnerable, a shining beacon of hope, while they are the darkness surrounding us, ready to lash out at any moment and drag us down. We must remain ever-vigilant to ensure they do not strike again."

"Is there anything I can do to help?"

"Not until you finish your training. It would be irresponsible for me to ask you to join the fight before you're ready."

"I already joined this fight when they kidnapped me and attacked the Tower," Emma protested. "There's no going back from that." The nightmares certainly hadn't gotten the message and stopped.

Alivia shook her head. "There's a difference between a fight for survival and fighting as a mage guard or arch mage."

Emma conjured up the memory of the mage guards training in the yard behind the Tower. Soldiers trained to use magic, the mage guards stood as the first line of defense against magic attacks on mundane armies. A group of soldiers without a mage guard to support them would soon find themselves wiped out if faced with a powerful, rested caster. Mage guards, though, could hold back the enemy caster long enough for an archer to put an arrow through their eye or for the company to retreat if necessary. It was this very same utility that made mage guards high value targets, even above officers. Or so Ethan had told her in an excited voice one night as they studied for their exams. "I would like to be a mage guard." *True, she secretly wanted to be a professor, but she could always become one after serving as a mage guard, couldn't she?*

Alivia smiled. "I thought you might say that. Hoped for it, actually, but again, you have to finish your training before joining the mage guard corps."

"I can join at eighteen regardless, can't I?"

"Technically. but the training is rigorous, both physically and magically. I wouldn't want a girl with two years of training under her belt to get burnt out by the experience."

"I can't see that happening," Emma protested. "I'm in this for the long haul. I won't be forced out."

"No, I suppose you won't be," Alivia agreed. She sighed and forced a smile. "I will meet you and Kylie at eleven o'clock tomorrow morning in the entrance hall."

Emma knew a dismissal when she heard it. Standing, she bowed. "Thank you for inviting me. And Kylie."

Alivia nodded in response, leaving Emma to turn and leave in silence. It wasn't an awkward silence - Emma didn't think she could be awkward around the arch mage. But still, there were times when the arch mage reminded Emma through her actions that she was not her mother. Not that she needed one - she was seventeen now.

She returned to her chambers earlier than anticipated, but Isabelle wasn't back yet. The new head girl, Rosalinda, stood lecturing a pair of first years about something, though Emma didn't pay attention to what they were arguing about. She considered leaving and going up to the library, to study, but her mind still reeled from her exams and she wanted one day where she didn't have to study a book.

"Emma," Rosalinda said as Emma had entered the hallway, intending to make for her dorm.

Emma sighed and turned.

The prefect had dismissed the first years, who were even then scurrying away like rats being chased by a cat and studied her. She didn't speak for a long moment.

Irritation spiked in Emma. "Did you want something?" She grimaced as soon as the words left her lips, for she knew they had come out harsher than she expected.

The fact was not lost on Rosalinda, who raised an eyebrow. But she made no mention of it when she spoke a moment later. "I heard you are staying for the summer." It wasn't a question. She would have received a listing from the adviser of their house. She technically wasn't required to stay for the summer, and someone would be assigned to watch over the house in the event the prefects and the adviser left for the summer, but maybe she had decided to stay? "What made you decide that?"

Emma, her temper incensed once, bit back a sharp retort. What business was it of the prefect what she did or did not do? She wasn't a squirming first-year, despite it being her first year at the magical school. She and the prefect were likely the same age. The girl had had it out for her since being appointed to the post, however. *What is her grudge with me?*

Hormones often make teenagers make irrational decisions, even with regard to people they interact with and form friendships with.

My hormones are going to make me snap at you, Shadow. Shut up. She shoved the sensation of her artificial intelligence from her consciousness and focused on formulating a response, preferably a polite response, to the head girl standing before her. "Yes. I'm remaining behind. It would be too far for me to travel to Ironforge to see my family and make it back in time." *That and it would be too expensive. And do I really want to face them?* She feared her old town would seem quaint compared to the metropolis that was Tar Ebon. She would feel like a big fish in a small pond. That would result in the more attention on her, which was the last thing she wanted, in truth.

The head girl nodded. "Well, I am staying too, so if you need anything..." she trailed off and cleared her throat. "I'll be here."

That surprised Emma. The prefect had barely said two words to her all year, even before being raised to prefect, and now she was offering her support? Did she have an ulterior motive, or was she afraid of Emma, or what? *Probably the latter.* Many girls, and boys, for that matter, had shied away from Emma while passing her in the halls during the months following the attack on the Tower. She had done nothing further to warrant the fear, but apparently fighting down a large group of enemy mages in the basement of the Tower and winning warranted a healthy dose of fear. Never mind that she hadn't been alone in the basement - her friends had sacrificed much to give her the time to stop the

Cult of Rae. No, it was she, Emma, who had obtained a reputation that exceeded even that of Isabelle.

"Uh, thank you," Emma replied, not knowing what else to say to the offer of aid. She had no intention of taking the girl up on her offer, but it was the polite response. "I will bear that in mind."

The girl offered a smile that Emma interpreted as nervous before turning in the other direction and heading toward the opposite hallway.

"That was weird," Emma muttered under her breath. She made for her room and found her roommates had already vacated the room. Emma sighed. "So much for goodbyes." Granted, only one of her roommates had even given her the light of the day. If anything, the other two talked to her *less* after the attack on the Tower. No love lost there.

Emma laid back on her bed and closed her eyes, not ready for sleep but using the darkness to focus. A parade, and a dance to follow. There was no time to go shopping, so she would need to wear the dress she'd worn earlier in the year. *During a simpler time*. Who was she kidding, though? The time before the attack on the Tower hadn't been simpler, not really. It had merely had the illusion of being simpler. The reality was far different.

What would it be like to meet a queen? Alivia said she was more down-to-earth than other monarchs, but Emma still harbored doubts about that. She hadn't met the crown prince or any of the other royal children, so she truly had no basis by which to gauge the parenting skills of the monarch of Tar Ebon.

For a time she lay there, letting her mind wander in a thousand different directions. At last, some time after the sun had slipped below the horizon, sleep overcame her.

Chapter 3

The glow orbs high hanging high above the entrance hall illuminated Emma and Kylie as the bell tolled eleven times, indicating the time they were to meet Alivia. As if on cue, the arch mage emerged from the elevator, looking resplendent in a yellow dress, and approached them. "Are you both ready to go?"

Emma felt slovenly in her traveling cloak and school clothes, but she told herself she would get dressed properly before the ball later that evening. *There should be time before the ball, right?* She straightened her back and smiled. "Yes, we're ready."

Alivia nodded as if expecting the response. "Excellent. Follow me." She led them out through the main doors of the Tower and into the muster yard. It was vacant save for a few guards on patrol. Not surprising, given that most of the students had left the day before or at dawn. Even her brother had left that morning, though he and their friends had all said goodbye. Isabelle had made a show of shifting into the shadow realm, heading back to her father's ship, while Ethan and Richard and Melissa rode off in a carriage, probably to the steam wagon depot. In just nine months the steam engines had become popular, with lines going to more places to the east and south. *Nothing heading to the north or west yet, though.*

They passed through the main gates and joined the flow of people headed toward the main thoroughfare. The air held a vibrancy Emma had yet to feel, with most of the citizens wearing dresses or suits. As if the queen cared what her subjects wore.

At last they arrived at the edge of the crowd lining the main road through town. Guards lined it, facing the crowd to make sure the peace was kept, and the royal procession was protected.

"Do we get a special spot?" Emma asked.

Alivia snorted. "I'm not that special."

Emma looked back to Kylie. Her friend gave her a shy smile. She had been ecstatic to come along to see the parade, and to join her and Alivia for the dance.

"But," Alivia went on. "We do get to stand with the other mages."

Emma perked up at that and searched the crowd. She wasn't sure what she expected. Perhaps a cluster of well-dressed people? There were plenty of those - but they weren't composed of mages. Maybe the group in robes? No, those were priests of An'Hara, the goddess of fertility. "Where are they?" She asked at last, stumped as to their identity.

"There," Alivia answered, pointing across the thoroughfare to where a ragged group of men and women in a variety of clothing, including work clothing, dress robes and formal wear, stood. "I admit they're not much of a sight. Most mages leave the Tower during the summer break."

"So do we just cross the road?" Kylie asked. She peered one way and then another. "I don't see the parade yet."

"No, the procession hasn't started yet," Alivia acknowledged. "Follow me." She pushed through the crowd to the line of guards and said a few words to one of the guards, which Emma could not hear over the din.

The guard looked Alivia up and down, then eyed Emma and Kylie before stepping aside and waving them through. He pushed two onlookers back when they tried to follow through the gap, much to their chagrin.

Within minutes they'd crossed the stone river and joined the group of mages. A few nodded to them, while most ignored them. The full-fledged mages either liked Emma or ignored her - if they felt fear at her potential, they didn't show it. They seemed to treat Alivia similarly, though Emma suspected it was the mages who were intimidated by a strong arch mage that ignored her. They came to rest between two of

Emma's teachers just as horns echoed through the city and the sound of marching feet echoed distantly.

The first hint of the procession did not show itself for several minutes. At the head of the parade rode a man in gleaming gold armor accented with silver. A helm covered all but his eyes and a sword hung at his side. He sat atop one of the tallest horses Emma remembered ever seeing. "That must be a general," she whispered to Kylie.

"Indeed. That is General Ravenscroft," Alivia answered, somehow picking up Emma's words despite the crowd. "General of the Home Guard."

Emma didn't need to ask who the Home Guard was. She'd seen their members around enough to recognize them, and her brother had taken it upon himself to fill her in on the *entire* history of the order. They were the guardians of Tar Ebon, never leaving the city for any reason. Ethan stressed that even if a city two miles distant were under attack the Home Guard would not march beyond the walls. The idea of such a draconian policy struck Emma as odd but when she'd asked, Ethan explained the second rule - no army of Tar Ebon could enter the city proper. Only the Home Guard was allowed inside en masse. In fact, if two or more armies gathered outside the walls of Tar Ebon it would be in violation of the constitution and possibly be viewed as a coup.

Numerous other men, no women, not surprisingly, rode behind General Ravenscroft. They wore silver armor accented with gold, standing in stark contrast to the general. Emma didn't ask who they were - she assumed they were his lieutenants and other sub-officers.

Row upon row of horsemen came next - each in their dress uniforms and wearing feathered hats. They held sabers against their shoulders as they rode.

Pikemen followed, pikes tilted to the exact angle and marching in unison. Emma felt her heart swell and couldn't help but smile. It was one thing to see horsemen, but these were the meat of the army. They were the front-line soldiers who would fight, and die, in the name of Tar Ebon at the command of those fancy officers.

Archers marched behind the pikemen, bows unstrung but held against their shoulders, quivers hanging at their sides. They preceded a band composed of drums and flutes and brass horns and instruments Emma did not recognize. The upbeat tune they played caused Emma to tap her feet in time.

A second cluster of guards came, this time composed only of silver armor-clad soldiers with swords at their sides. The difference became apparent when rank-by-rank the mages lifted their hands and pillars of various elements, including fire, ice and what Emma saw as wind, erupted skyward. "Mage guards," she whispered.

Alivia did not hear her that time, but Kylie looked over. "That's what you want to be, right?" Emma had briefed her on the details of her conversation with Alivia from the day before that morning.

"Yes," Emma replied, unable to take her eyes off the procession, though the light reflecting off the silver armor made her want to shield her eyes reflexively.

"They look impressive. I wonder if they can fight."

Emma nodded in reply. The swords at their sides suggested they knew how to fight.

A cluster of men, and women, surprisingly, following the mage guards, caught Emma's attention. They did not wear flashy armor or sharp uniforms. Instead they wore dark brown cloaks with forest green tunics peeking out from beneath. They each wore a sword at their side and held bows much longer than the other archers in their hands. The quivers appeared to be on their back.

"Who are they?" Kylie asked.

"Rangers," Alivia responded.

"Rangers?" Emma asked.

"They primarily serve in the wilderness, preventing poachers and protecting travelers. It's rare for them to gather in one place, even for such a formal event."

"I wonder what brought them here," Emma said.

Her pondering was answered moments later when a man atop a black horse dressed all in black followed them. She recognized him immediately, even at a distance. "Dawyn."

"The supreme commander is also the ranger-general. In fact, it was his title before being raised to the rank of supreme commander in the Federation military. Before earning the rank," she amended.

Her amendment reminded Emma that she was looking at a war hero. This was the man who had charged toward the Krai'kesh crystal during the Battle of Pelinor Field and stabbed it with his blades, causing it to explode and nearly killing him with the impact. Emma wished she could have been there to see that day, though she feared she would have frozen in fear and died at the hands of a Krai'kesh warrior.

Dawyn seemed to recognize the cluster of mages, for he specifically looked over and gave them a two-finger salute before returning his attention forward.

What could be left? Emma wondered.

They had apparently saved the best for last, for knights in literal shining armor led the next procession. Their lances were pointed skyward, with small flags attached to the tips flapping in the wind. Even their horses wore armor. The four-column stream seemed to stretch for eternity before, several minutes later, it gave way to hundreds of soldiers wielding sword and spear. These were not the long pikes of earlier - these were shorter spears designed to be used in conjunction with a spear. Their shields were gold-plated, and the spears seemed to be protected by a layer of metal along the haft.

And then, finally, a carriage rounded the bend. It was an open-top carriage, though any would-be assassins would need to account for the ring of soldiers riding in tandem with the coach. Emma thought she recognized the emblem of mage guards among several. It made sense that mages would be present to protect the queen from magical assailants.

Inside the carriage sat a regal-looking older woman, who had to be Queen Coryn. She wore a gold crown that, while impressive, was not overly opulent. Not that Emma had seen any other royalty to compare the queen of Tar Ebon to. For all she knew, her crown was the fanciest of all the rulers. *I somehow doubt that*, she thought. *Anyone who calls themselves "emperor" likely has a large crown to fit the title.* She did not wear armor, instead choosing to wear a white dress that Emma suspected cost as much as a middle-class family in Tar Ebon made in a year. She waved at the crowd, her arm raised and her hand twisting ever so slightly so as not to tire her too quickly. She had half the city to traverse and thousands of onlookers to wave at, after all.

Several younger figures accompanied the queen, with the most notable being the young man across from her. His blond hair was cropped short and obscured by a crown even larger than his mother's. He wore a polished gold breastplate with silver embellishment while the pommel of a sword poked above the carriage.

"Who is that?" Kylie asked, echoing Emma's thoughts.

"The crown prince," Emma replied, remembering the stories she'd heard. "Neal." Being the eldest of the queen's children, Crown Prince Neal had no magic but was heir to the throne. His gender didn't matter, or so the stories said, for even had he been a girl he would have been next in line for the throne. *I'm glad he's not a woman*, she thought, eying his arm muscles.

She forced her eyes to survey the other occupants of the slow-moving carriage before it passed by. Next to the queen sat a girl Emma's age, with auburn hair and wearing a blue dress. Emma recognized her as Princess Feodora, second eldest of the queen. She'd seen her around the Tower but never spoken to her.

Next to Princess Feodora sat another girl wearing a red dress and looking only slightly younger than her older sister.

Next to Crown Prince Neal sat two boys as well, both looking pre-pubescent and relatively close in age.

Emma opened her mouth to ask Alivia about the other members of royal family, as she was curious as to their ages and names, when screams rose from the opposite side of the street. No sooner had the screams began than a hail of crossbow bolts arced toward the royal carriage. Several bounced off an invisible barrier Emma assumed was magic in nature, while a handful made it through and slammed into the side of the carriage. One of the boys, she thought it might be the crown prince, bent over, clutching at a bolt sticking out of his chest.

Chapter 4

"A ssassins!" a cry went up, whether from the queen's retinue or from the nearby mages she wasn't sure. In moments Emma felt surges of magic as every mage within range of her senses drew upon their magic. She joined them and felt waves of sensation wash over her. Multiple layers of barriers of air formed around the royal carriage, while the mage guards formed up behind rows of mundane soldiers with shields interlocking.

The thundering of hooves overwhelmed the sound of screaming and clattering of steel as Dawyn Darklance led his rangers, and dozens of the knights in shining armor, back toward the carriage. He leapt from his horse and raced toward the queen, seeming to move impossibly fast. "Defensive positions!" he roared, his voice likely being amplified by one of the mage guards.

They're already in defensive positions, Emma noted. *What more does he want? And what is he waiting for?* For once, Shadow didn't answer.

But the enemy, whoever they were, did. Figures appeared on the rooftops on both sides of the road, bearing crossbows. Their presence was not concealed, and they released their bolts with an urgency that suggested they knew death was imminent.

The bolts flashed through the air and again most shattered against the barriers erected. But to Emma's surprise at least three bolts made it through *all* the barriers, only being stopped by the wood of the carriage and, in one case, the flat of Dawyn's blade. *How are they doing that?* The barriers were meant to deflect all physical attacks. Could they be enchanted somehow? Hardened to withstand the impact with the barriers? After all, the barriers were just air solidified, but not enough to be opaque. There would be cracks that could possibly be exploited. Now

25

was not the time to be contemplating the theory behind their weapons - they were obviously partially effective. What to do about them was the question.

The crossbowmen tried to duck back from the edge, presumably to reload, but several were too slow. Fireballs thrown by mages, and arrows fired from rangers atop horses, struck their positions and they fell from the rooftops into the crowd, adding to the frenzy. It was all Emma could do to maintain her position as the panicked civilians fled around the group of mages. Had she not been in the cluster she would have been carried away, and possibly trampled.

"Someone get on those bloody roofs!" Dawyn roared. "Burn the houses down if you have to! Driver, drive, slowly! Soldiers, make a path!"

The carriage jerked into motion, with the troops shuffling to stay abreast with it and those in front of the carriage getting out of their way.

Why are they going slowly? Emma wondered.

It is a standard defensive formation, Shadow explained. *If the carriage were to charge ahead too quickly it could lose its escort and be ambushed far away from support.*

Oh, now you answer, Emma said, this time without annoyance. Could Shadow hear a tone in her voice? *They have cavalry, though. Surely they could keep up.*

That is correct. But cavalry cannot form an effective defensive line the way trained infantrymen can with shields.

Their shields don't seem to be doing much against those bolts fired from on high, she shot back, this time to no reply.

Fireballs heralded the next round of attacks from the mysterious enemy. They arced from beyond the edge of the rooftops and flared down into the crowd and splashing into the barriers. It was as if they *wanted* to hit the crowd. A distraction, perhaps? Create chaos so they could continue their attacks - or escape. Was killing the queen their goal, or something else? Why hadn't they led with the magic?

A loud moan emanating from the carriage caught her attention. The boy who had been shot - she could see now for certain that it was the crown prince, was leaning back in the seat, held there by two soldiers while a third studied the bolt sticking from his chest.

Emma walked out from the cluster of mages toward the carriage without thinking and almost took a spear through the chest as one of the soldiers stabbed toward her. Only a hand on her shoulder jerking her back saved her from impalement.

"Don't get yourself killed," Alivia scolded loudly.

"But I can help," Emma pleaded.

"They don't know that," she said, voice still raised to be heard above the crowd. "For all they know you're an assassin sent to finish the job." She sighed. "All we can do is protect them from outside."

"Not even you can get through?"

Alivia suddenly looked much older to Emma. "If things were calmer, maybe. But it's chaos."

Attacks of fire, ice and in some cases lightning surged toward the unseen attackers. Several balls of fire evaporated, ice melted, and lightning disappeared before reaching their intended targets, however. How many attackers were there?

Mundane arrows followed the Tar Ebon mages magical attacks, arcing over the rooftops and being blown into the sky like leaves in a high wind.

"Put your magic to good use," Alivia snapped. "Don't just stand there like a dolt."

The intensity of the rebuke snapped Emma out of the shock she felt at seeing an attack on the heart of the city that had been her home for the past nine months. A city that should have been impenetrable was suffering a massacre at the hands of God only knew. She focused her magic and added her efforts to the defensive shields. The royal family might not survive another rain of crossbow bolts.

Movement caught Emma's eye. A brown orb sailed through the air. It landed amid the people, a rope poking out of the top and burning down. Emma's eyes narrowed, then widened as realization set in and horror filled her. "What..."

BOOOM. The orb detonated, causing a ringing in her ears and throwing civilians, blood and body parts in all directions. More explosive orbs sailed through the air and fell among the disoriented parade onlookers. Before Emma could isolate them with her mind to grab them with her magic they too had detonated. Tears ran down her face as her eyes fell upon the corpse of a little boy, cut in half by the explosion.

Rage replaced sadness, anger burned the fear away. *Where did those come from? Shadow,* she added, in case he didn't know she was talking to him.

One moment while I search through your memory. The moment played back in her mind's eye and for a moment it felt like she was watching two different scenes - one the scene of the bombs slowly arcing through the air and the other the aftermath of the explosions. *They appear to have originated from windows here, here and here,* he said, marking the windows with red arrows in her mind. Even as the replay of the event faded the red arrows remained.

Emma pointed to the nearest marked window. "One of the bombs came from up there." She started toward it without waiting for confirmation that either Kylie or Alivia heard her. The crowd had continued clearing out, with people fleeing down alleyways and into buildings - anywhere to get off the street, which meant she didn't have to fight her way to the door. A glance back confirmed Kylie and Alivia following her. She briefly considered flagging down guards to follow them, but by then the culprit could have escaped. Time was of the essence.

The trio raced up the stairs, Emma referencing the mental image of where the bomber had lobbed the bomb. "Third floor," she said, breathing heavy. She had been keeping up with her exercise during her time at the Tower, but the events of the moment kept her on edge. They reached the third floor and looked around. The hall was empty, with all the doors shut.

"Which room?" Alivia asked.

"I...don't know," Emma replied. She closed her eyes, hoping that the memory would help her, but the exterior of the building was very different from the interior of the building and she had no frame of reference. All she knew was a general direction. "Right," she pointed down the hall to her right. "And the right side faces the street."

Alivia walked to the first door on their right and, without knocking, slammed the door open with a concentrated burst of wind akin to a strong man swinging a sledgehammer into it. Then, with lightning crackling around her fingers, she stalked in. She returned a few moments later and shook her head. "No one in there. Spread out. Check the rest of the rooms one-by-one."

"And if we find them?" Kylie asked, sounding hesitant.

"Shout for help." Without waiting for a reply, Alivia moved to the next door and prepared to repeat her assault.

Emma took up position in front of a door to Alivia's left hallway and was surprised by Kylie joining her. *Can't she get her own door?* "Stand back," was what she said instead. She focused her magic, preparing to imitate the battering ram of air Alivia had employed. Before she could strike, however, the door swing inward.

A sword swung toward Emma. She hurled herself to the side and heard the steel strike the frame of the door. "Help!" she shouted, struggling to rise and fearing she would be impaled from behind.

A wave of heat washed over here, accompanied by a scream. A lance behind showed her assailant on fire and he dropped a moment later.

Behind the charred corpse stood Alivia, glaring daggers at the man, as if she could kill him twice. Her expression softened when her eyes fell on Emma. "Are you hurt?"

"Just my pride," Emma replied, rising. "I froze."

"Me too," Kylie said.

"He caught you by surprise, that's all," Alivia said with a wave of her hand. "Follow me." She led the two girls into the room their assailant had occupied. Inside they found a crossbow leaning against the wall in one corner. The cries from the street below drifted in through the open window. "Looks like he worked alone."

"Or his accomplice already fled," Emma said. She pointed to a chair by the door. "There's a second cloak here." The first was hanging from the chair nearest the window. "And there's no sign of bombs."

"A decoy?" Alivia asked skeptically.

Emma shrugged, trying to grasp at the threads of her theory. "Perhaps one was the lookout? And when the first man threw the bombs the other man ran?"

"Leaving the second to die or be captured? And the man only had one bomb?"

"What if the second man was the decoy," Kylie asked. "The first man went somewhere else on purpose and this man was left to throw us off the trail."

"I like that theory better," Alivia said. "We need to find the other man, and fast."

Another series of explosions rocked the street out front. "Too late," Emma said, mouth growing dry.

Alivia led the two students out of the room and down the hall. She slammed open door-after-door but found them empty. At last they came to the final door of that building. A feeling of dread settled in Emma's stomach. She opened her mouth to suggest an abundance of caution, but the door burst outward before Alivia could do more than muster the air for her next attack, splinters of wood lancing out. Fortunately, the splinters struck Alivia's cluster of air and stopped, but not before a few hit her leg. She stumbled and cried out, falling to the ground. A bomb flew out of the now-shattered doorway and landed at Alivia's feet.

Emma felt her eyes grow wide and she thought fast. She had to save Alivia before the flame on the wick reached the bomb. *Think, Emma, think!* She could try to throw the bomb, but it would take too long to form the "hand" to grab it. She could try to surround the bomb with air and contain the explosion, but her barrier wouldn't be enough to contain the fragments and the heat. Nor could she pull Alivia to her quickly enough. Wait. The flame. She could...she reached out with her magic and encased the bomb in a thin layer of air. Then she evacuated the air from within the bubble. The flame, which had been moving along the wick steadily, started to dim. It made it another inch or so before snuffing out. Emma let out a sigh and resisted the urge to fall to her knees out of relief.

Alivia let out a sigh of relief and smiled at Emma. "Thank you." Her expression hardened as her eyes fell on the doorway. She stood, without any hint of uncertainty or wavering resolve but with a slight limp, formed a ball of fire in one hand and a shield of air in the other and stalked through the door. Emma followed and found a man being held aloft by the arch mage, a bomb still in his now-immobile hand and a match in the other, burning down.

"Who do you work for?" Alivia demanded in a voice that could have frozen a glacier.

The blond-haired man dressed in a black tunic seemed unable to move his lower body but turned his head to spit on the floor. "I ain't tellin' you nothin'." He sounded sincere in his conviction.

Alivia seemed to think so too, for an instant later the man flew through the open window and his scream was cut short moments later.

"Why did you do that?" Kylie asked, sounding astonished. "He could have been questioned."

"There's no time," Alivia said. "We couldn't risk leaving him here and he'd slow us down if we had to drag him along behind us. Now let's get back down there." She brushed past Kylie into the hall.

Emma stepped to the window and looked down. The crumpled body of the man lay there, blood pooling below. None of the people stopped. She searched frantically for the carriage and found it only a short way away from its position when they'd entered the building. Why wasn't it making more progress?

The answer to her silent question came a moment later when she first heard the clashing of steel and then saw the melee of armed men. The soldiers who had formed a ring of steel around the carriage were under assault from what at first glance looked like ordinary civilians. Only as Emma watched, untrained in combat though she was, that she realized they were trained combatants. Perhaps assassins? Soldiers sent in plain-clothes? Mercenaries? Regardless, they pressed the Tar Ebon line hard, even giving the knights a fight with polearms and spears of their own.

The supreme commander made no move to engage the attackers, instead standing at the center of the carriage, rotating slowly as if tracking every possible threat. Indeed, a much smaller gaggle of crossbowmen emerged to fire another hail of bolts and the three that passed through the magical barriers were cut in half by his dual blades. Counter fire came swiftly and took several more enemies down.

They're losing momentum, Emma thought. *They're running out of time to kill the royal family.* Already horns blew in the distance, summoning reinforcements. Once the Federation army mustered it would be over. The enemy had speed, surprise, confusion and cramped conditions on their side but wouldn't for long. If the carriage managed to fight its way to Teldral Square it would be safe from rooftop attack or ground attackers.

"Emma!" Alivia shouted. "Hurry!"

Emma shook her head to clear her thoughts and rushed after the arch mage and her friend. She scampered down the stairs and followed them onto the street. Alivia was looking east, away from the carriage. Emma followed her gaze and gasped.

Dark clouds, which hadn't been there minutes earlier, formed above the city to the east and approached rapidly. Even as she watched, they seemed to condense and grow thicker, if that were possible.

Chapter 5

"Cyclones!" Alivia warned before drawing on her magic. Emma followed suit and wondered what was happening. She tried stretching out her senses to view the structure of the cloud formation, but it was too far. The clouds continued to grow thicker, and then individual threads of cloud stretched toward the ground, like fingers from a hand. Now she remembered the term cyclone. She'd read about their presence during the Battle for Tar Ebon on Pelinor Field twenty years earlier. The mage Jason, whom Emma had met not even a year earlier, had summoned cyclones and Alivia had used them as anchors for her devastating lightning strikes. Something told Emma these were not the product of any friendly mages, however.

"How do we defeat something like that?" Kylie asked from the other side of Alivia. The wind had picked up, drawing stray papers and other light objects toward the cluster of cyclones.

"We have to cut it off at the source," Alivia explained. "We have to find the enemy mage who is summoning it. They must be exceptionally powerful, or have a summoning circle, to perform this magic."

Emma remembered her lessons on summoning circles - they were difficult to coordinate, and it required the other mages to surrender their magic to the prime mage. If a single mage was unwilling, the spell would fail. There were also horror stories of the prime mage being killed amid casting and the other mages being burned out. "Where do we start?" she asked over the din.

"Use your senses. There are strands leading down from the sky."

Emma closed her eyes and stretched out with her senses. There, high in the sky, strands of whitish-blue streamed down from the clouds like string from a balloon. They did not come straight down, however, but instead curved and became a single strand to the east. "East," she said.

"Yes," Alivia said, nodding. She'd apparently already surmised as much. There was time for instruction even amid a battle. She cast a worried glance at the cyclone before leading them off. No other mages were in sight, save the mage guards who were busy fending off continued harrying by guerrilla mages.

The trio pushed through the crowd and made their way down a side street, the direction of the strands like an after-image overlaying Emma's vision. They emerged from the side street and there was the source of the magic - a manor house.

Several mean-looking guards stood watch out front. They started at the sight of the three women, then seemed to question among themselves whether the trio was a threat. But when Alivia strode purposely toward them it answered their question and they drew swords and aimed crossbows.

"I don't have time for this," Alivia said. She held out her hand, fingers splayed, and lightning arced toward the guards in front of the manor house. It struck them and they twitched like puppets being yanked around by a puppet master. Smoke drifted off their corpses as they fell to the ground.

A burst of wind blew the door open and a volley of bolts answered from within. This time, Alivia summoned a ball of lightning and sent it drifting through the entryway. A *zap* sound emerged from within, along with the screams of the dying. She bent over afterward. "I'm not as young as I once was," she said.

"Let us fight in your stead, then," Emma said, putting a hand on her shoulder.

She shook her head firmly. "No. I will see this through to the end." She stalked through the open door and led her students past the fried corpses of more guards and up a set of stairs.

No more traps or guards challenged them on the second floor of the manor, though the question remained as to where the summoning circle was. "Left," Emma guessed, pointing to a set of double doors at the far end of the hallway. "That's likely the quarters of the master of the house."

"And it would likely have a wide window and view of the northern sky," Alivia said as way of agreement. "Let's go." Lightning crackled between her fingers as she approached the door.

Halfway there, the door shattered and wood splinters sprayed down the hall, propelled by magic. They flew like a hail of daggers toward the women.

Instead of using wind to knock the wood splinters off-course, Alivia banished the lightning and instead summoned a wall of fire. The wood passed through the impromptu inferno and turned to ash.

As the smoke cleared, a hulking man covered head-to-toe in black armor emerged from the wreckage of the door. He wielded a black kite shield and an equally black blade. Twirling the blade, he advanced, boots clinking on the wooden floor.

"Metal armor will not avail you," Alivia said savagely. The lightning returned and arced toward the man.

He raised his blade and the lightning ran down the black blade. But instead of the man twitching as the lightning fried him within an oven of his own making, it continued to run up and down the blade.

Emma's eyes widened. That shouldn't be possible. Everyone knew metal was a conductor of lightning, what Shadow called electricity. Unless...could he be using magic to hold the lightning within the confines of his blade? She would have asked Shadow for a scientific explanation if they were not fighting for their lives.

"Foolish woman," the man said in a deep, sinister-sounding, voice. "Do you think we did not foresee your presence? Doom has come to Tar Ebon." He pointed his blade toward Alivia and lightning arced from it faster than the eye could track.

Alivia caught the blast on her hand and directed it into the wooden planks at her feet. Even still, her hand started to blacken and the smell of burning flesh filled the air.

Knowing she had to do something to help, Emma summoned a ball of fire and hurled it, while Kylie summoned a spear of ice and sent it sailing toward the man.

The man lifted his shield and the fireball splashed against it and disappeared. The ice shattered against the black surface.

That must be a magic-infused shield, Emma thought. *Normal shields would have frozen or been pierced by ice and would have super-heated and burned him if hit with a fireball.*

Pardon me, Ma'am, but the material of his sword and shield appears to be mage-forged.

I've heard the term but, what is *that?* Magic-infused articles was a study for third years or above.

Mage-forged armor and weapons are bonded at the molecular level to be harder than any other material, even diamonds. A pair of mage-forged blades were used famously by Dawyn Darklance during the Battle for Tar Ebon to destroy the Krai'kesh magic nullification crystal.

I remember the story, Emma responded. *I didn't realize it was mage-forged blades.*

Only a moment had passed while Shadow had lectured Emma, but already the smoke from the fire had disappeared and the ice shards littered the floor.

The enemy mage guard laughed evilly. "Child's play. Now witness true power!" A ball of fire formed in front of him but instead of propelling it down the hall, he spun it into a horizontal cyclone of red-orange flames and shoved it forward.

The intense heat caused Emma to step back and the walls to smolder as the tunnel of twisting flame shot toward them. *I must do something,* Emma thought frantically. Fire was her specialty, after all. Closing her eyes, she felt the structure of the attack - a cyclone with air for its frame encased in flame. No, she was wrong. It was flame enchased in *air* - the opposite. The flames would be impossible to extinguish without first shattering the wind frame acting as the carrier.

A counter-barrier of air could block the attack, but with its speed chances were the flames would unravel against the barrier and scorch them. And there wasn't enough time to unravel first the outer layer of air and then manipulate the flames. It was notoriously difficult to control someone else's summoned elements.

Think, Emma, think.

The air cooled as Kylie tossed an icicle toward the oncoming inferno, but it melted halfway there, and water turned to steam instantly.

Alivia, likely identifying the same issue Emma had, summoned her own horizontal cyclone of air and sent it swirling toward the enemy attack. The two clashed but then Alivia's cyclone fell apart and the enemy's continued its slow progression down the hall.

The walls of the manor had started to burn closer to the dark mage guard. If the flames were not extinguished, the entire manor would burn down in short order.

An idea came to Emma, but she hesitated. *Don't be stupid, Emma,* she scolded. *You almost died doing this before.* Then again, that had been a year earlier when she'd been an untrained sixteen-year-old. A lot had happened since then, and her confidence had grown.

"Stand at my side," she warned as she stepped toward the heat. Raising her hand, she waited for the mouth of the cyclone to come within a few inches of her hand, then closed her eyes and *sucked* the air-encased flame toward her, willing it to wrap around her arm. Pivoting, she held her other hand out the other way, pointing back the way they'd come.

The enemy attack obeyed, twisting around her arm. She cringed from the heat but focused on holding it away from her skin and instead channeled it over her shoulders and down her other arm. The same cyclone flowed from her other arm and past her and her allies. Within moments, the cyclone was past them.

She inspected her arm, expecting to see charred skin, but there appeared to be no damage. *I channeled it properly, instead of absorbing it like the inexperienced me would.*

The black mage hardly seemed surprised at this turn of events, for he lifted his blade and the flows of magic showed him readying another spell.

Alivia looked worse for wear, her hand scorched and a look of pain clear upon her face. Kylie looked uncertain. *We're running out of time. We have to end this! I must end this.* She suspected his shield would block or his sword absorb any spell sent his way but...what if she could affect the structure of his shield? *Shadow, mage-forged shields...*

My records show mage-forged armor, weapons and shields are created by the compression of the molecules of...

I remember. But can it be undone? Can the compression be reversed with magic? The hint of an idea took spark in her mind.

Materials of this density can be susceptible to intense vibrations, which can cause the molecules to vibrate rapidly, causing immense heat.

What kind of vibrations? Her thoughts flashed rapidly between her and her implant, causing her perception of time to slow as she waited only a few milliseconds for Shadow to respond.

Vibrations caused by sound waves should be suitable.

But I don't have any musical instruments. Wait. She withdrew her belt knife and turned to Kylie. "Give me your belt knife."

Her friend wore a perplexed expression, staring at her without comprehension.

"Belt knife, now," Emma repeated.

At last Kylie withdrew her knife and handed it over.

The glowing around the dark mage guard's sword increased in intensity. She suspected he was going to unleash a lightning attack next.

Not wanting to waste any more time, she closed her eyes and slammed the blades of the belt knives together. A *ding* resounded, small at first, but with her senses she detected the sound waves pulsing down the hall like ripples crashing incrementally against the shore of a pond when a large object was thrown in. She banged them together again, harder this time, and more waves came, closer together and seemingly stronger. *So if I increase the intensity of the waves...*

She slammed the blades together again, but this time she was ready for the waves to resound out. Grabbing them with her mind, she condensed the waves while keeping them from dissipating. The result was a ball of sound encased within an energy field projected by her mind. She cast it forward and it slammed into the enemy's shield. At first, there was no sound, but their shield vibrated. Then the metal seemed to...melt, though she detected no heat generated. Continuing to push the orb, she pushed it through his armor and then, with one final push, through his body. She released the sound waves and an ear-piercing metallic *ding* reverberated through the hall as the evil mage guard tumbled forward.

Emma let out a deep breath, a sigh of relief, then felt exhaustion wash over her and felt the urge to topple over like her foe. Only Kylie's hand on her arm stopped her from falling.

"We aren't finished," Alivia said. She took a step and then toppled forward.

"Alivia!" Emma cried, falling to her knees beside her. "Are you all right?"

The arch mage didn't answer, moaning and then falling silent, unconscious.

Chapter 6

"Shit," Emma swore. She looked up at Kylie. "We're on our own." Her eyes went to the shattered door the dark mage had stepped out of. Now that his body was out of the way, she could see flashes of light coming from the room beyond. Their teacher was down, and they still had who knew how many foes to face in the room beyond. *But we must do it,* she thought.

The two approached the door and peeked around the corner. Five figures in black cloaks with hoods up stood in a circle around a single figure in the center. Their arms were raised, while the center figure pointed through a hole in the roof toward the sky. Streams of magic swirled up toward the sky, twisting and writhing like tentacles.

How can we disrupt six mages? They could crush us like bugs. Their sole was they hadn't been noticed yet and the enemy likely expected their champion to have taken them out. They had one chance.

"Lend me your power," Emma whispered to Kylie.

Kylie closed her eyes and grabbed Emma's hand. A moment later her magic flowed into Emma.

Feeling the surge of energy, Emma racked her brain on how she could disrupt the ritual before they killed her. She could try to throw fireballs at them, but she'd never split one into six. The same for ice shards. She didn't have as much skill for lightning as Alivia and doubted she could summon enough to kill them.

A story she'd heard from Alivia once came to mind. She and her allies had been on the hunt for assassins when an enemy mage surrounded their entire inn with fire. Only quick thinking on her part had stopped the fire from consuming the room they'd been standing in.

Everyone else in the inn died. *What if I could summon a ring of fire to surround these mages, incinerating them? But can I do it fast enough?*

To do it, she would need to infuse wind with heat and swirl it around them fast enough. But where to draw the heat from? *That's it - the heat from the hallway.* The walls had started to smolder during the enemy's attack, so they likely still held residual heat. She stepped back into the hall and closed her eyes, stretching out her senses. The residual heat in the walls glowed red to her mind's eye.

Casting out strands of magic, she drew energy from the pools of heat in the walls and formed it into a cloud of intense heat swirling around her. The air crackled red as it ignited. *Now to direct the heat into the room and surround them.*

Emma cast the now red-orange stream of super-heated air into the room and coiled it around the circle of enemy mages as fast as she could. The center mage could direct his attack toward Emma at any moment. She had to kill him before he could do so.

The first stream of magic stopped as an enemy mage screamed and started patting at his flaming robes. The master stream controlling the atmospheric phenomena wobbled but stabilized.

A second mage lost their concentration but didn't light on fire. Instead they sighted on Emma and began summoning their magic, then doubled over as if struck by intense pain in their head.

Emma wasted no more mental energy on the fallen foe and instead threw more of her energy into the encircling inferno.

A third mage caught on fire and finally the big skyward stream blinked out of existence. The remaining two mages in the circle slumped to the ground, clutching at their heads, while the center one looked around for the source of the threat. His eyes alighted on Emma and *he* was able to summon his magic. A concentrated stream of dense wind flowed toward her.

Forced to relinquish her control on the circle of flame, Emma shoved the wind into the stone floor. It cut into the floor and, with the mage's control on it released, the remaining wind swirled through Emma's hair.

"You," he sneered. "You cannot stop us."

"Why does everyone keep saying that?" Emma asked. "I just *did* stop you."

"Foolish child. I am but one piece on the board. Valdorf will crush you before you have a chance to move your important pieces."

"Over my dead body," she replied, trying to sound braver than she was.

He smiled evilly. "That can be arranged. Valdorf has use for you...dead or alive."

Emma shivered. To think that the dark lord would have plans for her specifically terrified her. She shook her head, forcing his words out of her mind. *Focus, Emma, focus. You might end up dead if he gets the jump on you.* Instead of responding, she focused on forming a new attack in her mind. She still clutched the two knives in her hands.

She slammed them together and sent another concentrated wave toward her foe. But he seemed to be far more adept than the dark mage guard they'd faced, for he banished the sound with a wave of his hand, shattering the waves into every direction and causing Emma to drop the blades and hold her hands over her ears as the waves reverberated off the walls.

The floor. Her eyes focused on the gouge in the stone floor her enemy's attack had formed. *What if I could use my magic to* vibrate *the stone enough that he fell through?* It was a long shot, but if she hit it with just the right amount of noise, it might work.

Bending over, she snatched up the knives again and slammed them together. She aimed the sound waves this time toward the floor at her foe's feet. The stone did not break, but instead started to *melt*. If her enemy knew what she was doing, he offered no defense fast enough to stop her. Within moments the stone beneath him had turned to a sludge and his feet sank into it like the quick sand she'd heard about.

When she did not bang the knives again and the sound waves dissipated, the stone returned to its solid state.

The enemy mage roared in anger but was unable to move. He could still cast, however, and prepared to in that moment.

Run, her inner voice said. It wasn't Shadow. *He's trapped for now. Run and get help.*

The thought caught her off-guard. She wasn't a coward, to run away from a fight, was she? But then she looked at Kylie, who looked as tired as she felt. And her thoughts went to Alivia, lying unconscious in the hall. They were in no shape to fight and she felt as though her power could be exhausted at any moment.

"Emma?" Kylie prompted, likely guessing her thoughts.

Run, Emma, the voice came again. This time, though, it was familiar...

Ethan? Emma thought. In the heat of the fight, she'd forgotten her connection to her brother through their implants. *What are you doing here?*

We were only a few miles outside of town when we heard the alarm bells. We rushed back as soon as we could, but we got held up by the gate guards.

Where are you now?

In the courtyard of the Tower. The supreme commander ordered every able-bodied mage to come here in case the enemy mages try to take the Tower in the confusion.

Why did you tell me to run?

I could sense your panic, he responded. *Like, serious panic. I figured it was a good idea to run from whatever it was.*

How brave of you, I said, trying to put a dry tone on my thoughts. *What happened to the brother who held the Staff of Agamar with me?*

He faced a whole basement of cultists, Ethan responded. *And almost died. Maybe I matured.*

Emma rolled her eyes but refrained from insulting her brother further and moments later dodged a fireball launched by her opponent.

"We run," she said, answering Kylie's query and racing back through the ruined doorway into the hall. "Help me with Alivia."

The two girls picked Alivia up by the arms and carried her down the stairs, careful not to bump her head on the banister or steps.

Alivia is hurt, she said through the implant to her brother. *Can you have the Tower send someone?*

What street are you on?

Damn, I don't know. We were in a manor and it had two stories and... Emma...is it only *two stories?*

Yeah...

Okay, that's Merchant Row. It's where the merchants who want to pretend their nobles live. They can't afford much more than two stories. I saw Isabelle and her mom around here somewhere, maybe I can have one of them come and get you.

Emma groaned. Isabelle's mother, Bridgette, was in town too? Isabelle had so been looking forward to heading back on the seas for the summer. She didn't even need to ask why they'd stayed behind - likely they'd heard the alarms and returned or even been waylaid before setting sail. *That would be good,* I replied. *Better some help than no help.*

Right now they're ferrying the wounded here for the mages to heal if they can. I'm sure they'll come get a wounded arch mage.

And Isabelle is our friend, I pointed out. *That should count for something.*

True, he replied.

Did...did Frederik come back too? She didn't want to sound too hopeful. She wouldn't want her friend, she refused to call him "lover," to be put in harm's way unnecessarily.

Nope, not a peep, he said. *Maybe he was too far away to hear the alarms.*

Didn't he leave at the same time as you?

Yeah but... her brother fell silent. *You know, maybe he couldn't hear it in the south. With the hills and all that.*

You're right, Emma said, wanting to believe the explanation her brother offered. *He would have rushed right back if he'd learned of the attack - I know he would have.*

One sec, I think I see Bridgette.

Emma and Kylie finally reached the ground floor and, limping past the many corpses Alivia had killed on their way in, stumbled out into the street. Emma shielded her eyes and took in the carnage before her.

Bodies littered the cobblestones, blood running down the cracks. Crossbow bolts and deep gashes indicated the cause of death for many of the civilians, while charring suggested lightning attacks for some of the others. Clearly the enemy mage still stuck in the building behind them had taken his toll on the city.

Alarm bells continued to toll in the distance. They'd been muffled while the trio were in the building but now they reverberated the air around them. Drums echoed in tandem with the bells, likely calling the Home Guard to assemble. Smoke swirled through the sky, blotting out the sun. *How much of the city is on fire?* Emma wondered.

Was that for me? Ethan asked.

Maybe?

Well, most of the city is on fire, he responded. *Jason is leading the mages to put out fires and counter the enemy mages.*

And Bridgette?

She's on her way. Just disappeared.

Moments later, a shadowy cloud materialized and formed into Bridgette. She wore hardened black leather armor and a strip of cloth hung down from around her neck, ready to be moved into place over her face at any moment. She glanced casually, almost dismissively, Emma thought, around at the carnage, then focused on the two girls and the unconscious body of Alivia. "What happened to you?"

"Mages," Emma blurted. "In that building." She pointed to it. "I killed all but the leader and two others, who fell unconscious when their connection was broken." Her words came out in a flurry and her heart raced.

"Take deep breaths," the woman said. "Then hold hands and be sure you're touching her," she pointed to the arch mage. "I'm getting us out of here." Her eyes flicked to the building.

"What about the enemy mage? I left him stuck up there, but he won't be held for long."

Bridgette's eyes snapped back to Emma. "Do you want your body added to the count? Can you be sure you'd kill him this time?"

"Well...no," Emma said, taken aback. "But couldn't you...?"

"Girl, I've been killing dozens of cultists since the bloody attack began." She sighed. "But I'm not a fountain of energy, or invincible. Leave him for the trained mages I'll bring back with me when I get you to safety."

"Oh." *So she's not going to just let him go. She just doesn't trust us to fight him and win. I don't blame her.* They were first year students and, despite their past exploits and heroics, had proved today they still had a lot to learn.

Emma took Alivia's hand and then Kylie's. "We're ready."

"You've shifted before," Bridgette said to Emma. "But you haven't," she directed that at Kylie. "Don't let go, girl."

Kylie swallowed but nodded.

Bridgette placed her hand on Kylie's shoulder and the world shifted to gray.

Chapter 7

The world turned from gray to color once more as Bridgette shifted the two girls and arch mage back into reality. They stood in the center of Teldral Square, which lay in front of the palace.

The sound of shouted orders and the screams of the dying assaulted Emma's ears, threatening to overwhelm her with its intensity. Soldiers rushed the wounded on stretchers up the stairs of the palace, while others walked out of the palace at an unhurried pace ferrying the dead away. Soldiers ringed the square while mages maintained a barrier, though Emma had her doubts as to how long it would hold against the enemy they faced.

"Emma!" the voice of her brother cut through the din. He stood a short way away, Richard at his side. He ran to her and wrapped her in an embrace. "I was so worried about you!"

"I'm fine," Emma said, returning the embrace and then separating. "Alivia is the one who was hurt. And you should have seen our enemies."

"I bet you put up one hell of a fight," he said, smiling. His gaze turned to Kylie. "Are you alright?"

Kylie blushed. "Yes, I'm fine too." She studied the cobblestones.

Emma frowned at that. Kylie wasn't normally so nervous around her brother. She shook her head and pushed the thought aside. "We need to get Alivia medical care immediately."

"I'm already on it," Bridgette responded as two men rushed over and lifted Alivia up. "Take her to the infirmary and tell the mages she is a top priority and to keep her stable until Jason arrives." When they had left, she turned to the twins. "You and Kylie get yourselves checked out. The boys can go with you."

"Where's Isabelle?" Emma asked. She had been hoping her friend was the one to come rescue them and now she was nowhere in sight. Ethan said he'd seen her.

"I sent her to bring her father back here. Alivia needs expert magical attention. And there are others." She looked wistfully toward the palace. "Too bad the crown prince is beyond even his ability to save."

Emma's eyes widened. "The crown prince is dead?"

"Yes. He died before I came to get you."

"I saw the bolt that struck him," Emma said. "It pierced the magical barriers around him."

Bridgette grimaced darkly. "Yes, and my brother is still trying to figure out how *that* happened. If you see him, stay out of his way. He is *not* happy." Without waiting for a reply, she moved off and disappeared into shadowy mist.

"What now?" Ethan asked.

"We go to the infirmary, like she said," Emma replied. Worry over Alivia ate at her, but she forced it aside as they ascended the steps and passed through the huge reinforced wooden doors at the top and into the palace.

The sounds from the courtyard died down, replaced by different sounds. Moans still echoed, though from farther off, and soldiers still marched around, but things seemed more organized in here. Servants rushed to and fro, carrying towels and basins of water and more.

A guard stopped them. "What's your business here?"

Emma, conscious of her current garb, explained who they were. "We're mages from the Tower. One of the arch mages, Alivia O'Leary, was just brought in."

"You're not wearing mage garb," he challenged. "How do I know you're mages?"

Emma sighed. While she understood the need for such security measures, it didn't make them any less unpleasant. "We can show you some magic, if you prefer."

"Yeah, I can summon a fireball," Ethan said. "Light some tapestries on fire."

The guard stiffened.

"He's joking," Emma said, eying a row of crossbowmen standing one level above them, crossbows pointed over the railing. She imagined one word or gesture from the guard questioning them would result in their being made pin cushions. "But what proof would you like us to offer?"

"Wait here," he ordered, what little warmth might have been in his voice gone. "And if you move..." he pointed to the crossbowmen, a silent threat.

Emma nodded and glared daggers at her brother, silently willing him to be quiet.

The guard moved to room off to one side and moments later was followed by a gray-haired, crooked nose mage in robes. Emma recognized him as Professor Spurling, their chemistry teacher. He lifted his spectacles to get a look at them. "Eh, what are the four of you doing here?"

"Alivia's been hurt," Emma blurted. "We need to see her."

"Are they mages?" the guard asked.

"Students," Professor Spurling said, as if that were a major distinction. "But yes, they have magical potential. They are even considered saviors of the Tower...by some." His tone suggested he was not one who considered them saviors.

"You may go," the guard said, making a sign with his hand. "The medical ward is that way," he pointed to a hall on their left. "Second door on the right - can't miss it."

"Thank you, sir," Emma replied, bowing for added effect. As her mother once said, it paid to be polite.

The guard, perhaps still miffed about Ethan's joke, grunted in response and looked sourer than before. Professor Spurling huffed and headed back to the room he'd come from. Emma had serious doubts that if they'd been there on a nefarious mission that he would have been able to stop them.

Following the guard's directions, Emma and her friends at last arrived at the medical ward. In there, the source of the screams was found. Patients lay scattered throughout the room while doctors in white coats and nurses in light blue uniforms bustled about. In one particularly gruesome scene, a doctor was amputating a patient's arm while two guards held him down.

Flows of magic filled the air as evidence of magical medical care being administered. One mage stood over a patient, hand on his chest as tendrils of magic penetrated them. Without being closer, she had no way of knowing what magic they were attempting - and they hadn't gotten to inner body magic yet in school - but she could imagine they were mending bones or internal organs.

"How can I help you?" a plump nurse asked as she passed by with an armful of bloody rags. "Which of you are hurt? Or are all four of you?" She looked them up and down, lips pursed.

"Ummm, none of us are injured," Emma began. "We're looking for someone."

"This isn't a parlor, girl. It's no time for visitors."

"But we want to help," Kylie chimed in. "We're mages."

"Well why didn't you say so?" She snapped her fingers. "Get out there and help where you can."

"We heard an arch mage was brought in," Emma persisted. "We would really like to..."

"I can't tell queen from arch mage in this place," the nurse interrupted. "And it doesn't matter either. Start helping or show yourselves the door." She strode off without waiting for their assent.

"Yes, ma'am," Emma said to her back, eyes scanning the room in the hope of catching a glimpse of Alivia. There were hundreds of wounded here, but she'd expect the arch mage to be given a special place. *Or maybe the crown prince.*

"Do you want to look around?" Ethan asked.

"And risk her ire?" Emma countered. "No thank you. Besides, she's right. If we can help the wounded, we should."

"But we haven't studied internal medical magic yet," Kylie pointed out. "We could as soon kill them as heal them."

"They're dying anyway," Ethan pointed out, shrugging. "Could we make it worse?"

"*Much* worse," a female voice came from behind Emma, causing her to jump and spin around. Professor Riutort stood there, hands clasped behind her back, green eyes fixed on Ethan. "Let me tell you just how worse." She lifted one finger. "First, you could liquify their organs. Have you ever seen someone's lungs liquify and come spewing out of their mouth as they asphyxiate and die?"

"Uh, no?" Ethan said.

"Be lucky you haven't. That can happen if you use too *much* magic - it breaks down the cells of the organ you're viewing and causes it to liquify." She harrumphed. "You may have saved the Tower, and for that we are grateful, but here you are exactly what your lack of robes indicates - students."

"Could you teach us?" Kylie asked.

"Ah, the smart one of the bunch," Professor Riutort said, offering a small smile. "*That* is an appropriate question. And yes, I *can* teach you, though the classroom is quite...unorthodox. Follow me." She turned, revealing gloved hands covered in blood, and led them toward a hospital bed.

"Professor, we were told Arch Mage O'Leary had been brought here. Have you seen her?"

"I haven't, but I just had my hands up to my elbows in a soldier's stomach, so I might have missed her entrance. Was she seriously injured?"

"Not on the outside," Emma said. "But she was injured in a fight against enemy mages."

"After this next patient perhaps we will try to find her. But remember, in a situation like this the life of one person, no matter how important, must be weighed against the lives of all the others. It hearkens back to the philosophical argument of whether it is better to save the life of a king, no matter the cost, or save one hundred peasants."

"Couldn't you do both?" Richard asked, speaking for the first time since they'd entered the palace. "Save the king and then the peasants?"

"You mean the peasants that are left," the professor said. "And yes, you could save the king and then save those peasants who are left. But that is not the point. Our society often places higher value on those in powerful positions or who are wealthy. The question then becomes, do certain people have inherently more worth than others?"

The argument made Emma feel uneasy. If it were she or her boyfriend, Frederik, would doctors choose to save him or her? Would they place the wealth and influence afforded to him by his father above her rather lowly status? Sure, she was a mage, but so was he. She shuddered at the thought.

"The crown prince died," Kylie began.

"Where did you here that?" the professor asked, sounding startled.

"From Bridgette Thorpe," Emma said, feeling a slight bit of pride that she knew someone so famous.

"Sad news," she replied, pace unchanged. "That means Princess Feodora will be next in line to the throne. So long as she survived too."

"I think the others survived," Emma said. "We saw them during the attack."

"Good. Now follow me." She strode off toward where a soldier lay with a bolt sticking out of his stomach. He moaned writhed in pain. "This man, obviously, has an abdominal wound. Can any of you answer how best to proceed?"

"Pull it out and apply pressure to the wound?" Emma asked.

"I was looking for a less mundane solution," the professor said dryly. "The lowliest battlefield surgeon can do that. What advantage does magic give us in such a situation?"

"We can delve deeper," Richard said. "And look at the wound beneath the skin."

"That is part of it, yes," she said as she placed her hands on the bolt. "Knowing what else lies around the bolt and what type of head it has can help prevent more damage being inflicted when we pull it out. But what else? What can mages do about such a situation that mundanes cannot? Quickly, he doesn't have much time."

"We can cauterize the wound," Kylie responded. "We can heat the air around the shaft and head and burn the blood vessels as we remove it from the wound. That will minimize blood loss."

The professor removed one hand from the bolt and snapped her fingers, pointing at Kylie. "Yes, that is one such solution. And it's the cure of choice today." Closing her eyes, she sent flows of energy down the shaft of the bolt. Emma closed her eyes to follow the flows with her mind's eye.

As suggested by Kylie, the air around the bolt super-heated and smoke emerged from the gaps of air around the blood-soaked wound. Then, the professor pulled the bolt out, slowly, as the smell of burnt flesh became more potent. At last it came free. Blood trickled out of the wound instead of spurting and moments later the opening of the wound seared shut as though someone had pressed a hot knife to it. The professor tossed the bolt to the floor. "As you can see, we were able to stop both the external *and* internal bleeding, something mundane surgeons would be hard-pressed to do without stuffing the wound with cloths until the bleeding slowed."

"So interesting!" Kylie exclaimed.

"I think I'm going to be sick," Ethan complained, making a gagging noise, though Emma was reasonably certain he wouldn't puke.

"It's important to note the bolt did not pierce any important organs. If it had, we would first want to repair the organ with our magic as we moved the bolt out of the wound but before we pulled it out completely."

"How do you stop infection?" Emma asked. She'd heard stories of people dying from infections that prevented healing and killed them from the inside. She worried that was what Alivia had.

"Skilled mage physicians can *see* the causes of infection and destroy them. *I* am not such a mage," she pointed, "but he is."

Emma looked. Jason Thorpe, Isabelle's father and Bridgette's husband, strode down the center of the infirmary. He hadn't seen them. "Is he the only one with that gift?"

"He's the only one documented in recent times. The ancient texts tell of the Founders being able to perform such magic, but until Jason came along the art was lost to time. I almost didn't believe such 'germs' existed until he created a 'microscope,'" she said the word strangely, as if it were a foreign dialect, "to allow us to see them. Then he trained us how to use our magic to see them without such instruments. And he spoke of creating substances that could kill such germs, for those mundane surgeons to use, but I've yet to see such things yet."

"Progress takes time," Emma said, quoting her mother, though her usage had been in relation to progress regarding women's rights. The blacksmiths of Ironforge, mostly male, had never treated her as their equal, despite how successful she was.

"And some things are better left out of the hands of lesser mortals," the professor said. "Come on, we have more patients to see."

Emma disagreed with the professor but held her tongue. There were no 'lesser mortals' in her eyes. Yes, mages were gifted with special powers, but that didn't make them inherently better people. Just looking at the mages following Valdorf was evidence of that. Also, how could the professor reconcile the idea that the lives of royals were no more valuable than peasants en masse and the idea that mages were superior? Would the life of one mage be more valuable than one hundred mundane peasants?

"Would you excuse us?" Emma asked. "We really need to speak to Jason."

"That's Mr. Thorpe to you," the professor said with a sniff. She paused. "But watching him could be a good lesson for you. If he doesn't need you, though, return to me. There are plenty of patients here who need help."

"Yes, professor," Emma said, then beckoned to her friends and headed off toward the eternal. "Jason," she said as she neared.

The man looked startled as he met Emma's eyes. "What...," he cleared his throat and slowed his pace. "I mean, yes?"

"Do you remember me?" Emma asked.

"Of...of course I do," he said, though he looked like he'd seen a ghost. "Emma, Ethan, Richard and Kylie. Friends of Isabelle."

"Yes. Your wife told us Alivia had been taken inside. She was injured fighting a dark mage. We were hoping you could attend to her."

"I was just on my way to see her. What you did, stopping that cyclone, saved many lives, I want you to know that."

Emma blushed. So Bridgette had told him what they'd done. "We were just in the right place at the right time."

"Well, right place or not, you allowed me to turn my energy from combating the cyclone to combating other cultist hot-spots, which saved lives. Your parents would be proud."

Emma thought that compliment an odd thing to say, but just smiled indulgently. "Thank you, I'm sure they will be when we tell them one day." She hoped she lived long enough to see them again.

"Ah, yes. Alivia. Shall we go?"

Emma held out her hand. "Lead the way."

Jason led them through the infirmary to a set of double doors at the far end. The guards saluted him, though they eyed Emma and her friends warily. They wore the livery of the queen, though that was no surprise with them being deep inside the royal palace.

"They're with me," Jason said which assured the guards enough for them to open the doors.

Inside, they found a row of half a dozen beds along the wall opposite the door. Only two were occupied. One body lay with a white sheet over it, while the queen knelt beside the bed. That had to be the crown prince.

Alivia lay in the second bed, looking paler than milk in the orange glow of dozens of candles lining the walls. Two mages in robes stood over her, one to each side, hands on her shoulders. Emma sensed flows of magic being worked, though she didn't delve further to see what they were doing.

Along the wall to her right sat several boys and girls whom Emma recognized as being the children of the queen. Among them was Princess Feodora, who seemed to be the strongest among them. Her somber eyes held silent strength as she met Emma's gaze, while the others stared at the stone floor.

Jason rushed immediately to Alivia's side, leaving Emma and the others to stand awkwardly in the doorway. She decided to make for the princess. They hadn't known each other well, what with the princess being several years ahead of Emma at the Tower, but they did have magic in common.

The princess, whose gaze had been drawn to Jason, shifted her attention back to Emma as she came to stand in front of her. She did not speak, seeming to appraise the group.

"Hello," Emma said stiffly. She didn't intend for it to come out like that, but what did one say to a queen? And it wasn't like she was some peasant, and they were no longer a monarchy, so was bowing appropriate? She offered a hasty curtsy and saw Kylie following suit out of the corner of her eye. Richard bowed and then nudged Ethan, who repeated the gesture. Emma felt sure she would hear something about this later from her brother.

"Hello," Princess Feodora replied.

"I'm sorry for your loss," Emma began. "We heard that your brother..." she left the rest hanging.

"He died," the princess finished. "Murdered by fanatics." The bitterness and anger in her voice was unmistakable. "Save your sympathies - I will have vengeance."

Emma's eyes widened in surprise at the vehemence and resolve in the princess's voice. Clearly her anger was growing out of any residual sadness she might have felt earlier. "If we can be of any assistance, we would be happy to help," Emma replied. "We're mages. First-years, but..."

"I know who you are," she cut her off. "Saviors of the Tower."

"We don't really like that name," Emma said as way of weak protest. "We weren't alone in saving it."

"Well, the history books have limited attention spans," she said. "They'll probably fail to even mention my brother." She pointed toward where he lay beneath the white sheet. The queen had yet to move from his side.

"I doubt that is true," Emma contested, though she probably should have kept her mouth shut.

"Time will tell," she replied. "Even the Founders are long forgotten by all but dusty tomes."

Not having a comeback to that, Emma looked over Feodora's siblings. A younger girl in a tattered red dress with blonde hair sat sandwiched between two younger boys in dusty navy dress uniforms. The oldest of the boys couldn't have been more than ten years old. "How are your siblings faring?"

"They're stronger than they look," Princess Feodora said defensively. "You should probably see to the arch mage." Her tone suggested the conversation was over.

Way to go, Emma, she thought, *making a princess hate you the first time she meets you.* "Good idea," she said aloud, then walked over to the bed where Alivia lay. She heard her friends' footfalls behind her.

Jason stood next to one of the mages standing around her bed. He held his hand on her stomach, eyes closed as flows of magic swirled around him and down into her body. He seemed to sense Emma's presence.

"Look at what I'm doing and follow along, if you can," he instructed.

Emma closed her eyes and opened her senses. She followed his flows of magic into Alivia's abdomen and gasped. Hundreds of blue and white streams of magic covered and penetrated the organs beneath the skin. "What's wrong with her?" she asked.

"She suffered internal bleeding as a result of strain caused by using too much magic," Jason spoke, sounding distant. "She used the remnants of her magic to try to control the bleeding and place herself into a coma-like state meant to protect her body. Now I am trying to repair the bleeding and any damage to her organs so she can awaken. But she needs nutrients, which is why I am infusing water taken from the air into her stomach to start, but she'll need food to restore her strength."

"So she can be saved?" Emma asked.

"I believe so. She protected her heart and brain and other vital organs by going into a sort of low-energy mode. But if she had sat without aid, she may have died. You did well bringing her here."

Emma felt a swelling of pride at knowing they'd saved the arch mage's life.

"Did you observe how I used my magic to carry particles of water through her skin and into her stomach."

"It's extraordinary," Kylie said, beating Emma to the answer.

"It's more cumbersome than giving her water by mouth, but she struggled with swallowing and I don't have the instruments necessary to insert a feeding tube or start an IV drip. If we were back at my lab, I would have more medical apparatus on hand. But it would be risky to move her given the circumstances."

"Do you think the cultists will strike again?" Ethan asked, sounding worried.

"It sounds like we still don't know how they got in, so yes, they could very well have sleeper agents inside of the city waiting to do further damage when our guard is down."

"Why didn't your wife do her job?" Princess Feodora asked.

Startled, Emma opened her eyes and turned to find the girl red-faced, glaring at Jason.

"She is supposed to have spies or whatever to keep the Federation safe from threats like this. Why didn't she see this coming?"

Jason sighed and opened his eyes, then met the gaze of the petulant princess. "My wife works hard to protect the Federation from more threats than you can imagine. But the Cult of Rae have had centuries to grow and are deeply entrenched."

"But..."

"Enough, Feodora," came the queen's firm voice. She stood next to the sheet-covered body of her son and gave her daughter a steady look.

Her daughter, who now stood with her back against the wall, didn't back down. "No! First Father, now Neal. Who's next, Salena?" She pointed to the girl sitting between her brothers. "Or perhaps Hadrian," the boy on the right of the girl, "or Tristan," the boy to her left. "How many more members of your family will die before our enemies are stopped?"

The sadness in her mother's eyes evaporated, replaced with anger. "I watched my mother, your grandmother, recount the death of my grandfather as he lay dying on a field having tried to stop the Krai'kesh advance. I watched thousands dye on the Pelinor Field as I stood safe atop the walls of this city, a young queen over a city under siege. So do *not*," her tone became sharp, but her voice did not raise, "speak to me of loss. We have all suffered, that is a part of living. And when the

Krai'kesh return, and they *will,* all of humanity will suffer." Her face softened and she looked old, resigned. "Now is a time for strength, Feodora. You will one day be queen of Tar Ebon - I need you to be strong too."

Feodora had the grace to look ashamed at her outburst. "Yes, Mother. I'm sorry." The words came out so soft Emma strained to hear them.

Through it all, Jason had merely watched. Now he nodded, closed his eyes and turned his attention back to Alivia. Perhaps he was used to such outbursts from his daughter and wife.

"Good," the queen said, nodding in satisfaction. "Now that that is settled, we must discuss another matter of import." She paused, waiting until all eyes but Jason and the other two mages were upon her, before speaking. "As Jason said, the threat the cultists present is very real and present. Feodora is right in that we can afford no more deaths within the royal family. With that said, I am sending you, Feodora, and your sister and brothers, north to Seaholme."

"Seaholme?" young Prince Tristan asked. "Where is that, Mummy?"

"It's along the Hagues River, Tristan," she replied. "It has long been a secret refuge for the Tar Ebon royal family. It was used once, long ago, and it shall be used again. You will journey there and take refuge until the threat has passed."

"You want us to flee?" Princess Feodora said, challenge inching back into her voice.

"I want you to be safe," the queen retorted. "And right now, safety means going into hiding. I do not see Valdorf's forces laying siege to Tar Ebon, they do not have that strength, or they would have done so by now, but they could certainly continue to be a threat to the royal family."

"And if I refuse?"

The queen sighed. "I would hope you wouldn't, but if you refuse then I'll order you tied to your horse."

The princess sniffed.

The queen turned her attention to Emma. "I would like to ask the four of you to go with her."

"Us?" Emma asked, taken aback. "Why?" *The princess hates me,* she thought. *Surely she'll reject my being sent along.*

"In the event something happens, I would rather have more mages with her. And with your ages, you will be inconspicuous and less likely to be noticed or thought a threat."

"I'm sorry, Your Highness," Richard chimed in, "but with the cultists on the loose, I am worried about my family's farm. I'll be heading east as soon as the gates re-open."

Her gaze flicked to Richard and she nodded. "I understand, young man." She turned her focus to Ethan. "And I presume you'll be joining him?"

Emma's brother swallowed hard, then looked to Emma.

He wants to make sure I won't be angry, Emma realized. She thought about speaking to him through her implant but chose instead to nod. *It was always the plan, and Richard is right, his family farm could need him.*

Ethan shifted his gaze back to the queen. "I am sorry, Your Eminence, but I will be accompanying Richard."

"It's 'Your Highness,'" Feodora put in with a sneer.

Ethan blushed but said nothing.

The queen smiled gently, avoiding looking at her eldest daughter. "It's the respect behind the gesture that matters, and a simple enough mistake. But what about the two of you?" This time her gaze settled on Emma and Kylie in equal measure. "Will you aid my children?"

Emma looked to her friend, who nodded. Technically, neither of them had had much planned for the summer, so it would be a nice trip.

"We would be honored to go," Emma replied. "If the crown princess has no objections."

"I'm not the crown princess yet," Feodora snapped.

The queen held up her hand, calling for her daughter's silence, then nodded. "*I* have no objections, and that is what matters. It is settled, the two of you shall accompany my family north."

"You're not coming?" Feodora asked, sounding concerned.

"Not immediately," her mother replied. "I will follow once I have cleared things up here."

"But by then it will be safe for us to return, won't it?"

"Please don't argue with me, Feodora. This is in your best interest."

"It feels like exile," she grumbled.

The queen chose not to respond to her daughter, instead clapping her hands. "You will leave on the morrow with a small entourage. We do not want to draw the attention of the cultists by sending too many troops with you."

Well, this is an unexpected turn of events, Emma thought. *I hope the trip goes as planned.*

A SHORT WHILE LATER, Emma stood again in Teldral Square, gaping at her Isabelle. "You don't want to come with us?" she asked.

"It's not that I don't want to go," her friend began, "it's that my mother insists that I go with her and Father. They've found a lead suggesting many of the insurgents from today's attack came in on ships with manifests showing they were last at the Citadel."

"So what, you have to investigate?"

"Exactly."

"But your mother could investigate without you. We're going with the *royal family*." She put extra emphasis on royal family, as if that would impress her friend enough to gain her agreement.

"It's not just about the investigation, Emma. She wants to teach me more about my power. We wouldn't want a repeat of last year."

Emma recalled when she and Isabelle had accidentally gone into the shadow realm, and when they'd gone to the technologically advanced fortress near the roof of the world known as the Halls of Light. Only her mother's timely aid had rescued them. "I suppose being in school didn't give you much time to train with your mother, did it?"

"No, it did not, and I'm going to need to learn as much as I can if I'm to be my most effective against the Cult of Rae."

Emma sighed. Kylie had returned to the Tower in the company of Ethan and Richard, but Emma had remained to wait for her friend. She hated to be separated from her, as they'd become quite close over the past few months, but she knew it had to be. "I understand. I'll try not to be too sad." She smirked to show she wasn't completely serious about being sad.

Her friend smiled, then gave her a hug. "We leave this evening, and you leave in the morning," she said after they'd separated. "This may be the last time we see one another for some time. Good luck."

"You as well. You and Kylie feel like sisters to me, so I'll miss you dearly."

"Be grateful. You'll be up north where it's cooler. I'll be at the Citadel during summer - not a pleasant time with all the heat and humidity."

"I would have thought you'd be used to being by the sea by now," Emma replied. "Surely it's always humid on the ocean."

"Not always. The air can be dry when we're near the storm wall. Father says it's because the storms pull in the moisture as fuel."

"Well, I'm sure you'll manage," Emma said. She looked around at the gathered soldiers still guarding the square. How long would they be remaining on high alert like this? *Let us hope they don't attack again so soon after their last attack,* Emma thought.

Chapter 8

Emma's butt hurt. In all their travels, they'd rarely ridden horses, and now, after three days on the road, hers hurt.

I can engage your repair nanites, if you wish, Shadow said in her mind. *To eliminate the saddle sores.*

No, that would just make them come back, Emma replied, though she was sorely tempted to take her AI up on the offer for temporary relief. *I would like to know how much longer to the Haguesfort, though.*

Unfortunately my navigation is unavailable right now. However, based upon time since leaving Tar Ebon, and assuming an average speed of...

Cut to the chase, Shadow, Emma though. Sometimes the precision of her AI annoyed her. She just wanted the answer.

I estimate we are six days from the Haguesfort at our current pace. Once I reconnect to the neural network, I can give a more precise timing.

Great, six more days of this. She wasn't accustomed to luxury - the trip from Ironforge to Tar Ebon had broken her of any expectations of comforts in the wilds - but it *had* been over nine months since she'd left the city of Tar Ebon. She'd become more of an urbanite than she expected during that time. Now, going back to sleeping on the ground aside a campfire, riding a horse for hours on end, gathering water from streams they passed and using the bushes as a toilet seemed unfamiliar to her. *Oh how short my memory is.*

Something Shadow had said struck her as odd. *How long has your connection been down?*

Twenty-four hours and sixteen minutes.

Great. Does that mean I can't contact Ethan?

That is correct. All remote communication functions are disabled. I do not see what is 'great' about that.

It's sarcasm, she said while heaving a silent sigh. *It means the opposite of what I said.*

Ah, yes. I shall endeavor to add this expression to my lexicon.

Great. That was sarcasm too. Being unable to contact Ethan, or anyone, would limit their ability to call for help if trouble befell them. Not that she *expected* trouble to find them, but she didn't have great luck in the avoiding trouble category.

Kylie looked over at her, unaware of her friend's silent conversation but perhaps guessing. "Are you alright?"

Pushing fears of being attacked from her mind, Emma forced a smile. "Yes. Just feeling a bit chilled from the cold shoulder *her highness* is giving us." She purposely raised her voice for the last half of her response so as to be heard by the woman riding a half dozen yards ahead. Three days and the crown princess had said perhaps a dozen words to them.

Her siblings had been nowhere near so standoffish, with her younger sister choosing to sit with them at night and ask them questions and her brothers including her and Kylie in their boyish teasing. Only their older sister, and the dozen guards, who were expected to remain professional, remained aloof.

For the crown princesses' part, she jerked in her saddle and half turned her head, as if she were going to turn and give Emma a piece of her mind. But she thought better for it, or at least that it was beneath her, and instead lifted her chin as if to stare at the clouds.

"You shouldn't antagonize her," Kylie said in a normal tone. "She's going through a lot."

"Her siblings are just fine," Emma shot back.

"Yes, but none of them are the crown prince or princess all of a sudden," Kylie rebutted. "Try to put yourself in her shoes."

"All I can think is how much that would hurt my feet," Emma said. "I don't do well in heels."

"You know what I mean," her friend said with a serious look on her face. Strands of her hair twirled in the wind behind her. "Imagine if you lost Ethan."

Emma tried to picture such a tragedy but had trouble. Her brother had been with her since birth - they'd shared every day of their lives together for seventeen years. *She's right - if I lost Ethan I would be devastated.* She sighed. "Fine. I see what you mean, but still...she won't talk to me."

"What I'm saying is give her time," Kylie clarified. "Be open to becoming friends if and when she opens up. Can you agree to that?"

Emma pursed her lips. It *was* a pretty reasonable request. "Yes, I can agree to that."

They rode in comfortable silence for several more hours as the sun made its way toward evening. A north wind cut through the warm air, making baking in the sun all day more tolerable. The same wind would make for chilly conditions in a few hours, though.

A plume of dust on the road ahead caught Emma's eye. It materialized into a rider, one of the two scouts, as he reined up in front of the captain. Blood soaked the shoulder and arm of his tunic and an arrow point stuck out of the shoulder. Emma closed her eyes against the sight. *Come on, Emma, be brave. It's just a little blood.* She reopened her eyes as the captain looked this way and that.

"Bandits on the road ahead," he declared to the group, his eyes scanning his troops. "McNelson was killed. Verickson, see to Anderson." He indicated the wounded scout and the mage guard of their entourage nodded. Verickson was the only mage guard in the unit and doubled as the medic.

Emma leaned close to Kylie. "Maybe you can help."

"I think we might have bigger problems," Kylie muttered. "The guards seem worried."

Indeed they did, their heads turning this way and that as they scanned their surroundings. North of Tar Ebon, copses of trees gave way to vast swaths of farmland and eventually the open plains of Rovark. But they were not in Rovark yet, and the trees closed in on the road. Could the bandits attack them from multiple sides?

As if on cue, a horn echoed from *behind* them. Emma, startled, fought to regain control of her horse.

A second horn, identical in tone to the first, came from ahead of them, in the direction the scouts had said the bandits lay.

It's a trap, Emma thought.

"Your Highness, we need to get to safety," the captain said, addressing Princess Feodora. "There is a town a few miles up the road where we can seek shelter."

"Isn't that through the bandits?" the princess asked. She sounded confident, her back straight, but Emma felt sure if she looked at her face, she would see fear or concern.

"We'll have to fight our way through, yes," the captain confirmed. "But our scout confirmed there's only about a half dozen or so ahead. We don't know how many are coming from behind, so this option is better than sitting waiting here for them to tighten the noose."

"You're the expert," she replied. "Lead the way."

"Move out!" he shouted.

The wounded scout, having been bandaged by the mage guard after he cauterized the wound with conjured flame, ranged ahead. Four guards rode behind girls and royal family.

Twenty minutes later they were still in the woods and had found no trace of the bandits. No horns had come either to announce their presence.

I have a bad feeling about this, Emma thought.

They neared a bend in the road when their scout came surging into sight, waving his hands frantically. He'd made it halfway to them when two mounted bandits wielding crossbows rounded the bend and fired.

Before anyone, mage or non-mage, could do anything, the two bolts struck the scout in the back. He tumbled from his horse.

A waste, Emma thought. *He just got patched up, only to be sent back into danger. But I guess that's part of the job.* He'd risked his life to warn them of the impending bandit attack.

Already the guards were forming up, lifting shields to protect their charges. Eight in front, four behind, with the captain and mage guard behind the front guards.

The two bandits reigned up their horses and reloaded while the rest of their retinue joined them. Six bandits against a dozen guards, a mage guard and three mage students - they didn't stand a chance. So what were they trying? Surely the captain thought it seemed odd, didn't he?

"Get your magic ready," she called, intending it to be for Feodora and Kylie. "They may need help."

Feodora turned to glare at her, but then Emma felt magic swirling around her, ready to be used.

She may not like me, but she knows good advice when she hears it.

The bandits, lined up in a row, charged ahead. The two with crossbows sent bolts flying ahead of them, but they deflected off an iron shield.

Emma drew upon her magic but held back from attacking. Sure, she could have sent a fireball hurtling in their direction, but the bad feeling still nagged at the back of her mind and she wanted to conserve her energy to be prepared for anything.

The mage guard showed no such restraint, lashing out with a swirling line of air that buffeted the bandits and knocked two to the ground while sending the other four veering to the side. Their line had been split.

They adjusted their course and in moments crashed into the mounted line of eight guards. Steel clanged on steel as they met in combat. One of the royal guards toppled over, while two more fell back under the fury of the attack before surging forward again.

The two who had fallen from their horses ran to join the fray, but the mage guard was ready and a pair of fireballs flew toward the newcomers.

The captain, seemingly satisfied that the defense from this end was under control, turned to the rearguard. "Keep an eye out!" he shouted. "Something doesn't seem right. It could be a trap."

So he isn't a dolt, Emma thought. *He has the same feeling I do that this could be a trap.*

The attack came, but not from the direction they expected.

A hail of bolts came out of the woods from the west, with two piercing the captain's armor in the side, one piercing his horse in the neck and two others slamming into one of the princes' horses. The captain and his horse toppled to the ground, both dying, while the prince's horse bucked and he fell to the ground. Only quick timing by his sister Salena, who leapt from her own horse, rolled and rushed to his side, kept him from being crushed by the horse's hooves.

"From the west!" Emma shouted, her voice joined by Princess Feodora at the same moment. *Now is the moment,* she thought as she drew upon her power and prepared a spell. A barrier of air, assuming the bandits didn't have magic-imbued bolts like the cultists in Tar Ebon had, would give them precious moments.

Their foe chose that moment to blow the second horn they'd heard earlier, and the thundering of hooves causes Emma to turn. There a dozen more bandits rode straight toward them.

They have us surrounded, Emma thought. *Awfully sophisticated bandits.* She put aside the thought that they could be more than bandits for later. Regardless of their identity, they had made their intentions clear and deserved to die.

Maintaining the first barrier, she shouted to Kylie. "See to the wounded captain!" Then she pointed to Feodora. "Do something useful!"

The harsh words seemed to remove any hesitation from the princess, for moments later flames swirled around her and arced toward the southern attackers.

The mage guard of their company hurled fire toward the tree line where it disappeared against a...shield of energy.

They have a mage, Emma realized. *What bandits have mages?* It *had* to be cultists. The question was, how had they found them? They'd taken precautions - dressing the guards as common merchant guards and the royal family in trousers and tunics - to avoid attention.

Kylie ministered to the captain, and he screamed as she pulled the crossbow bolts from his side one-by-one and then seared the skin. It was a quick and dirty fix, and there could still be bleeding beneath the surface, but it would work for the moment.

The southern attackers are the biggest threat right now, Emma reasoned. They were a few yards from meeting the rearguard in combat - four against a dozen. She had to slow them down. She closed her eyes and prepared a spell to affect the ground beneath their hooves. *Sunder,* she thought, suiting magic to thought and forcing the earth to burst apart. She opened her eyes to see shards of dirt flying up toward the enemy formation. They slowed their horses as a cloud of dirt clouded their vision and scared their horses. Two horses reared and their riders fell. It wasn't much, but it bought them some time.

The enemy mage to the west launched a fireball and it slammed into Emma's barrier. Surely they could see the shield, so why had they done that? *To weaken me,* she realized. *They want to sap my strength.* She pushed more power into her barrier and concentrated on the north, where the original six bandits, cultists, whatever they were, were dead. But the royal guards had taken losses - only five of the original eight remained.

The captain ordered those five guards to form up on the western front, but before they could do so, a fireball arced out from the *east* and, to Emma's horror, exploded amid the five. Three scorched riders leapt from burning horses where they tried to roll in the dirt to no avail, while the other two were incinerated on the spot, leaving charred bodies to crumple to the ground.

Shit, Emma thought. That left three injured guards, who were likely to be dead soon, and four to the south. Then there was the captain and the lone mage guard. Plus the royal family and her and Kylie. They'd cleared the north, but now were surrounded on three sides. *We won't make it out of this alive if we stay here,* she thought. "We need to run!" she shouted over the din of clashing swords to the south. "Make for the woods!"

"Are you mad?" Feodora shouted back. She stood over her brothers and sister, who huddled on the ground at her feet to avoid being made targets. "Run *toward* the enemy mage?"

"I have a plan!" Emma shouted back. "Captain, can you and your men buy us some time? Captain?"

The captain, who stood gaping at his scorched soldiers, snapped his mouth shut and his eyes narrowed as he looked to Emma. "We swore to lay down our lives for the royal family. We will gladly buy them time to escape."

Emma inclined her head before turning to Feodora. "Get your brothers and sister up and ready to move. We're going east." She turned to her friend. "Kylie, get up."

"Maybe I should stay behind," Kylie said. "Help hold them off."

"You'll die if you stay behind," Emma said. "Besides, we need your help to escape." *And I need you,* she thought.

Kylie cast one more glance toward the captain before rising and joining Emma. "What's the plan?" she asked.

Emma joined the royal family and then outlined her plan. Once they were done, she clapped her hands. "Go, now!" She led the way toward the eastern wood line.

The enemy mage hidden there launched an ice bolt toward them.

Emma, having held on to her magic the entire time, deflected the ice bolt with a strong gust of wind, sending it slamming into the ground. "Dropping the barrier, now!" she shouted over her shoulder.

Kylie took advantage of the barrier dropping to hurl three balls of fire into the woods on the western side of the road. The last thing they needed was a mage following them. There was no guarantee her attack would kill the enemy mage, but the forest had caught alight, which would at least slow them down.

The remaining enemy soldiers to the south clashed with the remaining royal guardsmen, the sound of steel on steel and cries of pain and fury reverberating. The mage guard among them blocked an ice strike from the western mage with wind magic. Even with a mage guard, their chances of surviving against such odds were slim.

Emma reached the forest edge and almost took a sword to the gut as a cultist stepped out from behind a tree and stabbed toward her. She rolled to the side, distracting him long enough for Feodora to hit him with a fireball. As he rolled on the ground screaming, Emma scanned the trees, looking for the enemy mage.

Three more cultists wielding swords charged out from behind some trees.

Emma summoned lightning this time, frying her foes. The smell of burnt hair and flesh drifted toward them. *How many more cultists can there be?*

The enemy mage answered her silent query a moment later by stepping out from behind a tree a dozen or so yards away. He threw back his hood and held out his hands. A massive fireball formed between them and then he launched it toward Emma and her allies.

I can't deflect something that huge, she thought. Instead, she drew upon her magic and bound the ball of flame to the trees it passed with lines of energy. The heat transferred down the lines and into the trees. The anchor points on the trees smoldered and smoked and two trees caught fire.

Smoke clouded the air between Emma and the enemy mage. Taking advantage of the momentary obfuscation, she held her breath and charged straight toward him. Moments later, when the smoke resolved into his tall figure, she focused her mind's eye on the several rocks littering the ground. She lifted them up and hurled them toward her foe.

He threw up a hasty shield of air, transforming several rocks into puffs of dirt as they shattered into pebbles, but half a dozen slipped beneath the barrier and slammed into his ankles. He yelped and fell backward as his legs gave out. The barrier of air shimmered out of existence.

I have to be ruthless, Emma thought. *He would show no mercy to me.* Without hesitation, Emma evacuated the heat from a single point of air to the surrounding trees to form a ball of ice, then launched it toward the prone mage. It impacted his chest and his scrunched eyes widened as the super-cold orb froze his chest cavity and stopped his heart. He clutched his chest, fumbling his magic in a last desperate bid to reverse her attack, but he passed out before he could do more than stretch out to draw heat toward himself. Moments later, his chest ceased its rhythmic rise and fall.

Emma heaved a sigh and bent over. Her exhausted legs threatened to collapse while her head threatened to explode.

"Emma!" Kylie called, herding the royal family toward her friend.

Emma forced a smile. *Come on, push through the exhaustion.*

I can give you an injection of adrenaline, if you wish, Shadow said in her mind.

No, not yet, Emma responded. *I may take you up on that offer later, if we get into a pinch.* "Hurry, we need to move." The clang of steel on steel still echoed from the direction of the road, but she knew it would only be a matter of time before the royal guards were overwhelmed. "The guards mentioned a town north of here. We should make for that."

"Won't the bandits expect us to do that and intercept us?" Princess Feodora asked.

"Do you have a better idea?" Emma snapped. Did the princess really think that *now* was the ideal time to be arguing about where to take refuge. "First of all, they're cultists, not bandits. Bandits wouldn't be that organized. As for where to hide, perhaps we should fine a cave to hide in, or burrow into the ground? Or perhaps take refuge near the sky and hide at the top of the trees?" Her face burned.

"I..." the princess' mouth snapped shut and her cheeks flushed. "No...I don't have any better ideas."

"Good. Then stop contradicting me," Emma said. She could see what the princess was doing - trying to argue with everything she said as a form of resistance. "We head north." She oriented herself to the summer sun, to the south and west of them, then turned the opposite way. "We will have night on our side soon," she said, trying to put a positive spin on things. This close to the summer solstice, the sun set later in the evening, but still it had to be past eight bells.

The princess nodded, eyes downcast, while her siblings watched Emma with eyes wide.

They're frightened, Emma reminded herself. *They're looking to you, and the princess, for leadership.* "Let's move out." She trudged northward and five sets of footfalls heralded the obedience of the others. She considered running but knew that would likely tire them out before they reached the town. And with their foe likely having a few horses remaining, they could easily outrace them anyway. No, their advantage lay in making it through the night in the depths of the forest and arriving at the town by daylight after the riders passed. *If they pass and don't camp out in the town.*

A thought struck her then. What if they could throw them off the trail? A few of the trees still burned - what if she lit more trees on fire - to create a sort of fire break. She stopped, then stumbled forward as the princess bumped into her.

"Ow," the girl complained. "Why are you stopping?"

"Help me light the forest on fire," Emma said, looking both the princess and Kylie in the eyes in turn. "It'll create enough of a distraction to hide our tracks."

"It could also kill us," Kylie said. "Forest fires, especially in summer, can rage out of control."

"Emma's right," the princess said. "As much as I hate to admit it."

Emma raised her eyebrows in surprise. The princess actually *agreeing* with her on something? *What a shock.* "It's the only way, Kylie. We have to take the risk. We can blow the flames south, to avoid burning the town."

Kylie pursed her lips and stared into Emma's eyes for a long moment. Finally she sighed and looked around at the green-leaved trees all around them. "Fine. But let's hurry - I don't hear any swords anymore."

Emma stopped and strained to listen. She heard shouting, but no signs of combat. That suggested the enemy had eliminated the royal guards and were moving on. "Let's get started." Suiting action to words, she closed her eyes and focused heat into a single tree. It ignited. *That's too slow,* she thought. *And exhausting to go one-by-one.* Rays from the fast-setting sun poked through the trees. *It's worth a shot,* she thought.

She closed her eyes and directed her mind's eye to the pool of sunlight on the ground in front of her. Stretching out with her mind, she studied the twisting, pulsating waves that formed the light. *It's so strange,* she thought. *It's not like other elements I manipulate.* It seemed to be composed of particles of light, but they moved in wave-like patterns of gold-yellow. To further complicate matters, waves of heat undulated away from the line of light. *There's a reason only advanced students study light,* she thought. *It's the most complex form of energy to manipulate and an advanced field of study.*

Perhaps I can answer your inquiry, Shadow chimed in. *Light energy is a form of electromagnetic radiation. Light consists of photons, which are produced when an object's atoms heat up. Light travels in waves and is the only form of energy visible to the human eye.*

Ummm...I only understood about half of that, but thanks, Shadow. For unsolicited knowledge, she thought, trying to restrict that thought only to herself, though she wasn't sure if it worked. The word that stuck out to her was heat, and she planned to use the heat generated by the electro-something radiation to full affect.

She reached out with her mind and tried to grasp the photons which formed the ray of light, but it was like trying to cup water in a raging river - the light passed through her field of control as though it were not there. Frustrated, she tried again, this time to "push" the photons in the direction she desired. It was like a mundane trying to push the wind. *Wait, a mirror,* she thought, remembering how light would reflect off mirrors and windows and metal. *What if I could reflect the light toward the trees?*

A magnifying glass is a common tool for concentrating light in a single fixed point, Shadow informed. An image appeared in her mind, un-bidden, of a circular piece of glass through which objects on the other side, the bark of a tree in this case, appeared larger. Light hit the glass and focused into a pin prick on the tree. After several moments, the bark began to smolder.

So how do I create such an affect with my magic? Emma wondered.

Shadow's silence signaled his ignorance. He could describe phenomena in the physical realm with remarkable detail, but he had yet to show a firm understanding of how magic worked. Perhaps he was not programmed to understand magic. *A machine can't use magic, so perhaps that limits its understanding?*

Eyes still clenched closed, she focused her mind on the matter at hand, she envisioned the stream of photons like a stream of water. She could compress water through very narrow holes, so why not light? But water could be restricted by physical barriers, such as walls of air, but could light? She manifested a barrier of air in the path of the photons, but aside from dimming the light it did not stop it completely. *If I condensed the air enough, maybe that could work?* She flooded the space with more air particles until the density increased to an unprecedented, for her, level. The photons stopped and a pool of light formed on the surface of the air wall. *But no reflection*, she thought, disappointed.

How could I condense the light? She cocked her head to the side and studied the barrier of air. What if she poked a hole in the barrier? She hollowed out the center and a beam of like poked through, hitting the dirt again. But light still hit the barrier and didn't flow through the hole.

I don't have any glass here to focus the light. But what if I used my magic to direct the light? It stood to reason that if her magic was a form of energy, it could be used to create a tunnel. *And if I narrow that tunnel gradually, the light will become more and more focused,* she thought, the epiphany surprising her. *But I need to hurry.* Already she'd wasted time standing there like a dolt, even if it were only a few moments. The enemy could find them in seconds.

Conjuring what felt like the last of her energy, Emma disbanded the barrier of air and instead created a funnel of her raw magic, the extension of her mind that performed the manipulation of matter and energy. Her energy funnel, like its physical counterpart, matched the width of the stream of photons. But then, with each passing inch, the funnel narrowed until Emma could barely make out the end of the funnel. Then, the tricky part, to *twist* the tunnel toward a tree. She twisted it up and past one of the princes until the tip of the funnel pressed against the bark of a tree. Light shined on the bark. *Come on, work.*

At first, nothing happened. Emma held her breath. If this didn't work...there! Smoke rose from the point where the light struck the tree, followed by flames. Within moments the puff of smoke became a billow and then a torrent as the heat of the concentrated light consumed the living wood. Satisfied that the flames would not extinguish, she swiveled the hose directing the light and extended it to another tree. A few heartbeats later, that tree was alight. Three more trees followed in rapid succession. *Five trees are a good start.* She opened her eyes.

Kylie and Princess Feodora gaped at her. *They* had seen what she'd done. "How..." Kylie began.

Emma shrugged. "I'll explain later."

"We lit two trees on fire," Princess Feodora offered, pointing to where two trees smoked.

Emma nodded, animosity toward the princess set aside for the moment. They had a common enemy, and a common goal - to escape. "Good. Let's take advantage of it and move now."

Chapter 9

The sun had dropped below the horizon before the village the captain had spoken of came into view, illuminated by the light of the full moon.

"What do we do?" Kylie whispered from her side as they crouched just inside the tree line.

"I don't know," Emma admitted, squinting to make her friend out in the gloom. "We could go, but we don't know whether the cultists are already there or not. They could be waiting to spring another trap."

"I for one am tired of sleeping on the ground," Princess Feodora proclaimed from a few feet behind them. "And we lost our sleeping sacks during the attack."

"Oh, I'm sorry, Your Highness," Emma snapped, rounding on the princess, goodwill from before temporarily forgotten. "We should have hauled the bloody *wagon* with us through the woods, just so you could be comfortable!" The words came out in a furious hiss. *She* at least understood the danger shouting at the mouth of an open field could bring. "Forgive your lowly servants for the oversight."

"I..." the princess stammered, taking a step back and gaping at Emma.

"Emma," Kylie warned. Her voice seemed to say, "calm down."

"No," Emma said rejecting her friend's warning. "The princess has been whining during this whole journey through the woods. Perhaps it hasn't hit her yet that our *lives* are at stake."

The princess snapped her mouth shut and balled her hands into fists but held her tongue, choosing instead to stalk off into the darkness. Her younger sister looked back-and-forth between Emma and her sister before following. The boys huddled on the ground near a tree, trying to stay warm as the cool of night surrounded them.

Emma glared for a long moment, daring the princess to show her face or come back to argue, but when her verbal sparring partner did not appear, she let out a frustrated sigh she'd been holding. She didn't *like* fighting with other girls, but the princess just ground her gears. She looked to Kylie, whose eyes reflected the moonlight. "I know, I know," she said, trying to forestall her friend from scolding her.

Kylie wasn't going to let her off the hook, however. "I wish you and Feodora could just get along."

"I don't want to fight you too," Emma said, trying to get out of the conversation.

"You wish I would hate her too?" Kylie asked.

Emma winced. *Yes, kind of.* "No," she said instead, "I don't *hate* her. I just..."

"You're jealous of her," Kylie said.

"...Yeah...I guess I am," Emma said, realization dawning that her friend's observation was accurate.

"You're a peasant, Emma, and she's a princess. It's understandable to be jealous, but you need to get over it."

"I'm the daughter of a blacksmith," Emma shot back, "not quite a peasant."

Kylie stared at her.

"Okay, okay, I get your point," Emma conceded. "Maybe I am jealous...a little."

"The first step to reconciliation is admitting you have a problem," Kylie said.

"Wise words," Emma observed. "Though I have doubts as to whether you thought them up yourself."

"It's the thought that counts," she hedged.

Despite being hunted, despite watching many of their protectors die in an ambush, despite her arguments with the stubborn crown princess, Emma found herself smiling wide and chuckling. "Yes, I suppose it is," she said. "And besides, I quote my parents all the time."

"Which can get a little old after a few dozen times," Kylie said. She held up both hands in a "don't blame me" gesture. "Hey, it's the truth."

Emma opened her mouth to reply when the snort of a horse and the thumping of hooves drifted to her ears on the wind. "Shhh," she hissed instead, crouching and turning.

Torches illuminated horsemen thundering toward the sleepy village. Judging by the four torches spaced throughout the column, and a lone rider with a ball of flame glowing above his outstretched hand, there were likely eight or nine bandits and the enemy mage.

Shit, Emma thought. *I had hoped the mage guard would take out that enemy mage before dying.* It was rude to think ill of the dead, yes, but she couldn't help but think what if. *We're not going into the village tonight.* "Go tell the princesses to keep quiet, and *no* magic," she ordered Kylie. She waddled to the two princes. "Can you two stay as quiet as possible?"

The two boys nodded, eyes wide with fear in the gloom.

The riders entered the village and within moments loud bangs echoed from the town. *They must be knocking down the doors to the houses, Emma thought.* Unintelligible shouts drifted on the night air, the contents of which Emma could imagine. "Where are the girls" or "where are you hiding them," were the likely demands being made by the cultists.

After an indeterminable amount of time, silenced settled on the town and the glow of torches bounced northward. *They're moving away from the village,* she realized. Then she narrowed her eyes. Or were they laying another trap?

Princess Feodora and Kylie approached on hands and knees. "Psst," Kylie began. "What happened?"

Emma filled the two girls in on what she'd seen. "I'm wary, though. I think it could be a trap."

"So do we just wait out here until morning?" Kylie asked.

She probably asked to avoid Feodora asking and setting me off again. "I think that would be prudent. Then we can easily see the cultists if they come back." *When they come back,* she amended in her head. "Let's head further back and start a campfire."

Emma and her companions walked several hundred feet from the tree line before they found a clearing large enough for their party. Working in pairs, with the boys remaining in place by the, the girls gathered sticks and piled them high, then Feodora lit the campfire.

As Emma warmed herself by the fire, her thoughts turned to her brother. If she had encountered such adversity, had he too? It worried her that Shadow had been unable to reach him. *I hope you're safe, brother.*

SEVERAL HOURS, AND three rotating sentry shifts later, Emma arose from her place on the cold, hard ground. She rubbed at her side, where multiple sticks had stabbed into her with a vengeance, as if they were angry at her incursion into their land. Only ashes remained of the fire.

Kylie still sat where she had been when she relieved Emma three hours earlier. She smiled. "All was quiet."

Emma nodded, knowing that such a report was expected. If there *had* been an attack Kylie would have warned them or they would have been in captivity or dead by now. "Good," she said.

The royal family lay huddled on the ground, centered on Princess Feodora.

I shouldn't take pleasure in this but... "Wake up!" Emma shouted.

The princesses and princes jolted awake and rolled in multiple directions before standing and looking around. "What? What is it?" Feodora asked, eyes wide and magic swirling around her.

"It's morning," Emma said, maintaining a straight face.

Feodora looked to where the sun inched over the horizon. "You couldn't have let us sleep a little longer?"

"A band of cultists are out for our blood. Now is not the time for your beauty sleep."

The princess sniffed. "You could use some beauty sleep."

Is that a joke? Emma thought. *I should be upset but...I think that's the first time I've heard her make a joke.* She ignored the remark and pointed to the village. "The cultists haven't returned, so hopefully we can get there and seek shelter before they come back."

"*If* they come back," the princess said.

"They'd be stupid to not come back."

Five minutes later, after they had relieved themselves and gathered their belongings, they set out from the wood line toward the small village.

Emma's head swiveled this way and that, searching the horizon for any sign of dust rising in the sky which might herald the coming of mounted riders.

They made it to the edge of the village unbothered by anything but the warm sun. A surprising number of villagers walked the streets, women carrying baskets on their arms and men carrying one tool or another. A pair of horses plodded down what passed for a main thoroughfare, pulling a wooden cart loaded with bales of hay.

"Let's find the inn," Emma suggested, reading the building signage as they walked. It felt odd being the leader of their ragged band, as though she were usurping the natural order of things in the former kingdom of Tar Ebon, but the crown princess had given no protest.

Villagers they passed stopped to stare at them. A few women pointed to them, and a gaggle of children ran circles around them, giggling and asking unintelligible questions over one another.

The town was built like a cross, and as they neared the crossroad, they at last found the sign for the inn - a mug of ale next to a loaf of bread. "The Bread and Stein. Let me do the talking," Emma said as she placed her hand on the door latch.

Inside, the cool air of the dimly-lit inn caused the hair on Emma's arms to stand up. A portly, balding man stood cleaning a clay stein with a towel. He looked up as they entered, hand stopping its cleaning motion, eyes narrowing and lips pursing, but said nothing.

Emma cleared her throat. "Greetings."

"What do you want?" he asked in a gruff voice.

Emma had expected the response and forced a smile. "We are seeking rooms for the night."

"Day just started," he grumbled. "You gonna stay in your rooms all day?"

That was the plan, Emma thought. Not wanting to risk being on the road, they had considered laying low for several nights. Fortunately the princess had a pouch full of gold coins, so they could afford it. "Do you have any rooms available?" she asked, side-stepping the question.

He resumed cleaning the mug in his hand while he appraised the six guests on his threshold. "You got coin?"

"Yes," Feodora spoke up, moving past Emma and jingling her coin purse. "We can pay."

He sighed. "This wouldn't have nothin' to do with them riders who came through in the night, would it?"

Emma bit her lower lip, contemplating her options. They could lie, but then he wouldn't trust them when the truth came out. They could tell the truth, but what if he were in league with the cultists?

"Some very bad men are chasing us," Kylie chimed in, taking the decision out of Emma's hands. "We can pay for a room and would be grateful for a cover story should they return."

"I don't want no trouble," the innkeeper said. "You should leave."

"But..."

"Leave, before I call my boys to help you move along," he said sternly.

"But..." Emma stammered.

"I am Crown Princess Feodora," Feodora began, stepping forward, chin up. She reached into the satchel at her side and removed the tiara from within. "I am on a secret journey. We were beset by bandits on the road and took shelter in the woods. The royal family would be eternally grateful for your aid."

The innkeeper's eyes, which had widened as she spoke, narrowed again. "How do I know that's true?" he said, slight quaver in his voice. "You could have stolen that, or it could be fake."

"Do you really want to take that chance?" the princess asked.

That wasn't part of the plan, Emma thought. Word that the crown princess was in town would spread like a town fire during mid-summer.

"And who are they?" he asked, pointing to everyone behind Feodora.

"These," she gestured to her sister and brothers, "are my siblings." Her hand moved to encompass Emma and Kylie. "And these are my...traveling companions."

Way to downplay us, Emma thought. Granted, they weren't really friends, but she could have at least called them her guardians or protectors or something. That *was* their role.

The man nodded, setting down one stein and picking up another. Then he burst out laughing, a deep, booming laugh. "Ha ha ha," he said. "Well, Your Highness, I'm the emperor of Rakosh. Pleased to meet you."

Feodora's cheeks turned beet red in moments and her fists clenched. "This is *not* a joke," she said through gritted teeth. "We're telling the truth."

"Sure ya are," the innkeeper replied, chuckling again. "Best joke I've heard in a while."

"We have money." Feodora shook the coin purse again. "We can pay for rooms."

"Probably stolen money, lass. Don't want no trouble from the likes of thieves."

Thieves? He thinks we're thieves? "What did the cul...riders yesterday evening want? Who were they looking for?"

"They said they were royal guardsmen and were looking for traitors to the Federation. Said they were thieves. Described four girls and two young boys. So I'm giving you one more chance to walk away before I send word to them riders that you're here."

"Fine. Let us work for you for the night," Emma said.

"Don't need more help, lass. 'Specially not from thieves."

"We aren't thieves!" Feodora screeched, clenching her fists. Magic flared around her and she held out a hand, summoning flame. "Could common thieves do this?"

The innkeeper's eyes widened. "Mages. Are you all mages?"

"The three of us are," Emma replied. "And we don't want any trouble. We are mages in training at the Tower and we are telling the truth."

"I don't know...," he began.

"Do you really want to take the chance that we aren't who we say we are?" Emma asked. "What would the queen do to you if she heard you gave her children up to her enemy?"

"There's five royal children. You say you're the crown princess. What happened to the crown prince?"

"He was slain during the attack on Tar Ebon," Feodora said. "Has word reached your village of the attack?"

"No, 'tis the first I've heard of it."

"Well, those riders you encountered last night are cultists in the Cult of Rae. They want nothing less than the complete destruction of the Federation at any cost."

The man pressed his lips together and stared at a corner of his inn. Finally he shook his head. "I knew there was something funny about them riders. Fine, I believe you are good folk, even if I don't believe you are royalty."

"So you'll provide shelter for us?"

Come on, just say yes, Emma thought.

"If you got the coin like you said you do."

"And will you let us work here? Just until we figure out a plan?"

"I could use a few more serving maids for a night or two," he said, stroking his chin. "And them boys could help back in the kitchen."

"We agree," Emma said before the princess could respond. *The last thing we need is her reconsidering because it's lowly work.*

Feodora nodded. "We'll take the work."

"Good." He turned to the board behind the bar where keys hung. "I can rent you two rooms."

"That's fine," Emma said. *Kylie with me and the siblings with Feodora.*

He held out the keys. "I'll give you a few minutes to put your belongings upstairs, then get back down here. My kin and I gotta teach you some things before the evening rush comes."

The six travelers climbed the stairs and found their rooms at the far end of the second story. Emma counted four other rooms along the hall, but she couldn't tell whether they were occupied or not. *The innkeeper and his family probably live here, right?*

The door creaked open when Emma pushed on it after turning the key, and she and Kylie entered. "Well, I've seen worse," she said.

"It's better than the forest floor," Kylie said.

"You're always the positive one."

"Someone has to be."

They dropped their few meager belongings on two of the four beds crowding the room. A wash basin sat against the wall on their right, while a single window overlooked the back alley behind the inn. *I've been spoiled with indoor plumbing at the Tower*, Emma thought as she spotted the chamber pots beneath the beds.

Emma looked to Kylie. "How are you holding up?"

Her friend quirked her lip. "I'm trying to keep it together. But it's just a constant stream of bad luck for us. For me."

"Hey, I was having bad luck long before you came along," Emma reminded her. "If anything, the bad luck is following me and you're just around for the ride."

"Haha. I wonder how your brother and Richard are faring."

"Maybe they got out from under my bad luck umbrella," Emma said.

"Have you...heard from him?"

"No. My implant isn't working for some reason. I mean, it's working, but it can't connect to Ethan or anyone."

"Doesn't that scare you?"

Emma shrugged. "A little, but nothing I can do about it now, right? We have more immediate problems to address." *Like the fact our lives are on the line here,* she thought.

"I guess," Kylie said.

"Let's check on the others," Emma suggested, suiting action to word and making for the door to their room. Once in the hall, she knocked on the royals' door. "You all right?"

The door swung open and Princess Salena stood there. "Feodora is upset about the conditions of our room."

"Our stable boys live in better conditions!" her older sister grumbled from the other side of the room.

Emma rolled her eyes. *This is going to be long trip, assuming we make it out of this village alive.* "At least it's clean...enough...and it's safe."

"And it's not the woods," Kylie said.

"How can the two of you be so optimistic?" Feodora asked.

"We've been through a lot." Emma held up her hands. "And we're not trying to brag. But compared to being in Cultist custody, this is a walk in a field."

Feodora frowned. "We should never have agreed to come on this trip. Mother should have never sent us on the trip."

Emma suppressed a sigh. *Princesses.* "You can take it up with her when you see her again. Until then, let's focus on surviving, shall we?"

"Fine," she said, arms crossed over her chest.

Emma nodded. "It's settled then." Without waiting for the others, she headed for the stairs. Gradually footsteps heralded the others following her lead.

The innkeeper, who had still not given them his name, leaned against the bar, arms crossed over his chest, giving them appraising glares as they tromped down one-by-one. "Line up straight," he ordered.

Emma's cheeks flushed. *Is this an inn or the military?* Still, she and her friends complied, forming a semblance of a line. A ragged line.

"Now...if you're going to work here..."

Chapter 10

Three days. For three days and two nights Emma and her companions had served at the Bread and Stein. She, Kylie and Feodora had served the patrons, while Salena helped in the kitchen along with her brothers.

The innkeeper's daughters had expressed joy at having help - it meant they could skip out to be with the boys they had their eyes on - or so Emma surmised based upon the snippets of conversation she had overheard.

It was the eve of their third day in the village of Deyman's Grove and Emma found herself scrubbing beer and picking up clay pieces from the dirty wood planks that formed the floor of the inn. Two patrons, one a traveling merchant, the other a local, had started fighting minutes earlier. The innkeeper and his eldest son, Theodore, had broken the fight up in short order, and thrown the two men out into the dying light, but not before a stein or two of beer, and the accompanying clay ware, plummeted to the ground.

Feodora walked by, back stiff as a board, nose up in the air, as she carried two mugs to a table across the aisle. Emma resisted the urge to shake her head. *Three nights and the princess* still *turns her nose up at this work. It's not glamorous, but it's providing cover until we can form a better plan.*

What little time they'd had to plan had proved unfruitful. They could head back south, on foot, with no horses, in the heat of summer, to Tar Ebon. Or they could do the same, only heading north, in the direction the cultists had gone. Or they could go east or west, which would be even more pointless since they'd soon find themselves wandering aimlessly in the wilderness. She'd heard plenty of stories back home in Ironforge of travelers trying to take a shortcut to Tar Ebon or Rovark and never being heard from again.

With no appealing options, and no reliable or trustworthy way to send word back to Tar Ebon, they were floating on a proverbial island surrounded by a sea of forests and fields.

They'd received some strange looks the first night working there. Some villagers had looked at them with longing and tried to slap or pinch their butts as they passed, while others enjoyed tormenting them with frivolous orders. Night two had consisted of more of the same, only this time with different patrons. But now, on night three, the leering and pointless tormenting had mostly subsided as she and the other two girls had ceased being exotic.

Kylie, in contrast to Feodora, stood next to a table, blue apron covering a plain gray dress the innkeeper's wife had found for her. Her own melodious laughter joined with the raucous laughter of the patrons occupying the table. Unsurprisingly, she'd also collected the most tips of the three girls.

I don't hate this work, Emma thought. *I'm just not a people-person.* Which was true enough. She had friends - a close circle - but was not one to stand in front of a room full of people and speak. The same philosophy held true waiting tables; she felt outside her comfort level approaching strangers to ask what they wanted to eat and drink.

The door to the inn slapped open as two broad-shouldered Rovarkians stomped in. Their entrance drew eyes from several patrons - eyes that turned downward to search for secrets in their cups or in the bread on their plates when they saw the men.

Emma froze. *I recognize those two.* Cultists. *Focus, Emma. Act natural.* She forced her arm to keep moving and her eyes to focus on the grain of the wood she scrubbed. *If I pretend I belong here, they might overlook me.*

Feodora, however, made no such attempt to blend in. She took one look at the men and gaped for a long moment. Then magic flared and began gathering heat for a fireball.

Kylie chose that moment to walk by Feodora and take her by the arm. She tugged and the magic evaporated, then continued to lead the princess toward the kitchen.

Emma let out a sigh and watched the men out of the corner of her eye.

The men scanned the room slowly, stopping on nothing in particular. The first stopped on Emma for a split second longer, then moved on.

"Anyone seen four girls and a couple boys come through here?" the second cultist asked in a booming voice.

The patrons, still admiring the cutlery, tabletops or drink ware, shook their heads.

"Oi ain't seen no travelers," one graybeard man said, stumbling to his feet. "But there's pretty lasses here in the inn." He raised a gnarled finger and pointed toward Emma.

Shit, Emma thought, sweat trickling down her back. She forced a smile and turned to face the two men. She chuckled. "I'm just a lowly serving girl, kind sirs," she said. *Please believe, please believe.*

"A serving girl with a nice butt," the old man shouted before cackling madly.

Both men scrutinized her, looking her up and down and causing her to shudder involuntarily. "Where'd the other two serving girls go?" the first cultist demanded.

"To fetch urgent orders," Kylie's voice came from the rear of the inn. Emma turned and found her friend carrying a platter filled with bowls of soup, while Feodora trailed behind her, face contorted in a mix of disgust and rage, carrying two pitchers in each hand.

"You sisters?" the second guard asked.

"Yes," Emma said, at the same time Kylie said, "no."

"I mean," Emma stammered, "we are like sisters. But not blood sisters."

"Humph," the first guard grunted. He looked to his partner, who shrugged. "If any of you see some strangers passing through, four girls and two boys, you send word north. Understood?"

"Of course, sir," Kylie said, affecting a poor imitation of a curtsy. Feodora remained standing, though she had the sense to direct her eyes to the floorboards.

Emma nodded hurriedly and followed Kylie's lead with a curtsy of her own.

With a grunt, the first guard led the way out of the inn.

Emma released a sigh she didn't realize she'd been holding. *We fooled them.* She stood there dumbfounded for several more moments, as if expecting the cultists to return any moment with reinforcements, but when no enemies entered, she turned to her friends.

Kylie was in the midst of passing out bowls of stew or soup, while Feodora filled mugs.

The floors can wait, Emma thought. She made her way to the kitchen.

There, the innkeeper's wife, Ivet, stood chopping vegetables at a table, while Salena sliced cuts of meat into smaller chunks. The boys were nowhere to be found. "Where are the boys?" Emma asked, eyes widening and heart thumping.

"They are out back with Jakub," the thin woman responded without turning around. "Helping to bring in more barrels of beer. Did the riders leave?"

"Yes, the cult...I mean riders...left," Emma said. *Shit, I think I said too much.*

Her fears were confirmed a moment later, as Ivet turned toward her and pointed her knife at Emma. "Cultists? Is that what you meant to say, girl?"

Emma nodded while avoiding her gaze.

"And they're after you?"

"All of us, but yes," Emma replied.

Ivet sniffed. "Perhaps you *are* royalty like you claimed."

"I'm not royalty," Emma protested. "Feodora and her siblings are."

"Does it matter? They want you all dead, do they not?"

"I suppose," Emma said, shrugging. It bothered her to be compared to royalty, though. She came from humble beginnings and liked to think she would never be as pretentious as Feodora, even if she became an accomplished mage-guard one day.

"Then...," her words were cut off by a loud bang echoing from the dining room.

Emma felt the surge of magic from Kylie and Feodora a moment before a chorus of male, and a few female, voices drifted through the door, filled with surprise and anger. "Get the boys!" she snapped to Salena, then raced into the dining room. She passed the doorframe and found a stand-off in progress.

Half a dozen cultists stood in a line at the front of the inn, shields raised and swords at the ready. In their midst stood a man in black robes who emanated magic.

The dark mage from the forest, Emma thought. *The mage-guard with us must have failed to stop him.*

The dark mage threw back his hood and smirked. "You cannot achieve victory," he said in an oily tone. "My master has need of you."

"Well, your master obviously didn't tell you he was sending you after three mages," Feodora said, flaring her magic as a sword master might brandish their sword.

Their foe chuckled. "Three child mages are of no concern to me. You will submit willingly, or you will be made to submit." He flared his own magic and Emma gaped at his power. Had the woods been merely a test? No, she closed her eyes and opened her mind's eye. Two flows of magic streamed from outside, through the open door, and into the mage in front of them. *He has help.* But why lie? Surely they would sense their presence as soon as they started casting.

"We have to join our powers," Emma called out to the others.

"We've never done that before," Kylie called back.

"Yet more things you *children* are lacking in. Do not fear - my master will provide proper instruction for you."

"Your master can go to Hell!" Feodora said, casting a fireball toward the man.

He deflected it with contemptuous ease, absorbing the heat into a ball of his own hovering above his hands. "Fool girl. Let me show you the true power of a mage!" He drew heat from the air within and without the inn to form an extra wide ball of fire. It drifted not toward Feodora and Kylie but instead to a cluster of villagers who had taken shelter behind an overturned table, as though that could shield them.

Feodora tried to deflect it, but his control was too strong and it stayed its contemptuously slow course, as if he were gloating at how powerless they were to stop him.

"Give me your power!" Emma shouted, more firmly this time. "It's our only hope!"

Kylie complied, casting a stream of magic toward Emma. She savored it, feeling warmth flood her muscles and bones like a steam room.

"Feodora!" Emma shouted.

Too late. The ball of flame impacted the table and flames licked toward the ceiling. The villagers raced away from the burning wreckage, seeking refuge behind the bar.

Feodora stood stiff, magic still flowing around her, but not attacking.

Rather than call out again, Emma stormed toward the princess and grabbed her upper arm in a vise grip. "Feodora! We have to combine our powers!"

"It's too much," Feodora mumbled. "He's too powerful."

Emma resisted the urge to slap the fool girl. Now was not the time to freeze. *He's toying with us. He could have cast a dozen fireballs by now, and not slow ones. What is he waiting for?*

"Listen to the princess," the dark mage said. "You cannot match my power."

He has orders to take us alive, she realized. *He's not supposed to hurt us, so he's intimidating us.* Could she somehow use that to her advantage? She released her grip on Feodora's arm. "If you won't join me, at least cover me." Before she could explain, she zipped straight toward the enemy mage, head bowed.

His eyes widened and he began to cast a wind spell designed to send her flying backward, but he was too slow.

Her head slammed into his stomach, while her arms wrapped around him. Her momentum carried him backward out the door and he tripped on the threshold.

Feodora, seemingly snapped out of her frozen state by Emma's action, hurled spells at the guards remaining in the inn.

Performing a forward roll, Emma made it to her feet and, still drawing power from Kylie, cast lightning toward the two mages powering the first. They jolted and slumped to the ground, their flows of magic ceasing to feed their leader.

She turned to face her remaining conscious magical foe when someone big tackled her to the ground. "Oof," she said with a grunt, her command of magic fleeing and her connection with Kylie severing.

A scraggly Rovarkian man with crooked teeth snarled at her and raised a knife.

"Don't kill her!" the enemy mage shouted.

Her assailant paid his leader no mind and reared his arm back.

A dozen spells flashed through her mind, but fear held her magic back.

A brown blur flashed from the corner of her eye and slammed into the side of the man's head. It came into focus - a crossbow bolt. His eyes rolled up into his head and he toppled to the side.

Emma turned her head to see who had saved her.

A dozen or more barded horses bearing knights in gleaming silver armor with lances leveled barreled down the dirt street toward the mounted and dismounted cultists clustered in the street. Atop a horse to one side of the oncoming tide of steel sat a man reloading a crossbow.

The cultists, caught off-guards by the charge, had no time to form a defense. Those on foot were impaled or trampled, while those on horseback were thrown from their horses from the impact of lances or cut down by the swords the knights drew after striking with the former.

The original enemy mage stood up and summoned his magic. Lightning crackled between his fingertips. He batted aside a lance and shocked the rider until they fell from their mount. He set his sights on Emma.

Emma, who had regained her feet, closed her eyes and thought of a spell she could use. *I should try light magic again,* she thought. *Like in the forest.* The sun was close to setting, but with her mind's eye she located streams of light still illuminating the town. Like before, trying to grasp the photons which made up the sun's light proved futile. *I don't have the skill for that yet. I'll have to re-direct it and focus it like before. But I must move fast - he's already forming a spell.*

Indeed, lightning crackled over her enemy's fingers as he prepared to attack again. Any second now he would attack.

What if, instead of trying to re-direct the light, I focus the light before it reaches him? She focused on the air behind him, through which the photons illuminating his person flashed, and condensed the particles of the air like before to form a narrow funnel. At first nothing happened, so she widened the funnel entrance to collect more light while narrowing the funnel tip, further compressing the photons. At last the light made an impact, for her foe screeched in pain, shock and anger before his cloak ignited, distracting him. As he beat at his cloak, one of the knights thrust a lance through his chest.

Emma heaved a sigh of relief before pointing toward the inn. "There are cultists still in there," she said.

Even as her words left her lips, the door to the inn opened and Kylie and Feodora walked out. Kylie's magic was still linked to Emma, while Feodora held hers. "We took care of the cultists within," Feodora announced. If she were surprised by the appearance of royal knights, she gave no indication of it.

Emma released her link to Kylie's magic and gaped. "You defeated six cultists in there?"

"She did," Kylie said, indicating the princess with a thumb. "She was quite fierce with her frost magic."

The princess smirked. "I *am* a fourth-year student."

"I guess it was good you didn't lend me your power," Emma said. "It would have left you defenseless."

Feodora held her smile. "Yes, it would have," she said in a smug tone.

The knights, who had formed a loose semi-circle around their location, parted in one section and a single rider, a female, judging by their petite stature and long, flowing hair streaming out from beneath the helmet, made their way through the gap. She removed her helmet and...the face of the queen appraised the situation.

"Mother," Feodora breathed, affecting a curtsy.

Emma and Kylie followed suit.

The queen inclined her head. "We are fortunate we found you in time."

"You knew we would be ambushed?" Emma asked. *I'll give her the benefit of doubt that she didn't know before we left.*

"Shortly after you left, we uncovered spies within the palace. Upon questioning them, we learned of a plot by the cultists to capture you while you were enroute to the safe location in the north. Rather than entrust this to forces which may or may not have been trustworthy, I decided to head north myself.

"We passed the scene of the attack on your caravan earlier today and pressed on in the hope that you had fled to this village. We were right." The queen offered a smile.

"Your timing was impeccable," Emma said, smiling in return. "We might not have held out without your timely intervention."

"Are you taking us back to Tar Ebon, now?" Feodora asked. "Now that the traitors within the palace have been neutralized?"

The queen shook her head. "Tar Ebon is not yet safe. Though we discovered some traitors, it seems the roots of the twisted tree that is the Cult of Rae go deep. I fear for your safety back at the palace more than I do even now, having been attacked here. At least here you have places to run - in Tar Ebon you would be easily cornered in the palace."

"Then why don't we hide somewhere else in the city?" Emma pressed. "At the Tower or in the sewers?"

"Eww," Feodora interjected. "I would never be caught dead in the sewers."

"Even if the sewers saved your life?" Emma shot back.

Feodora sniffed in answer.

"I see you've been getting along," the queen said dryly. "Where are the others?"

"The boys are out back," Feodora said. "I think Salena went back with them."

"Fetch them, please," her mother said.

"Yes, Mother," Feodora said, huffing and disappearing into the inn.

"Secure the rest of the village," the queen said to a guard with a red plume sticking out from his helmet. "Make sure there aren't any more unpleasant surprises waiting for us."

"Yes, Your Highness," the man said, inclining his head and proceeding to issue shouted orders to his soldiers.

"Do you need a medic?" the queen asked Emma.

"No, Your Highness," Emma said. A few scrapes from her rolling in the dirt hardly warranted bandages.

"Good. Then rest up and gather whatever belongings you have left. We're going to continue the journey north together."

Emma nodded and made her way toward the door. *Hopefully things will be easier now that the queen is with us.*

Chapter 11

Five days later the slate gray towers of the Haguesfort came into view. They'd run across no further insurgent attacks, and the villages along their path north had treated the royal retinue with the pomp and circumstance due to them. *A big change from how we'd traveled at the start*, Emma thought.

Their party passed through the wooden gates, horns heralding their arrival, and came into the courtyard. A tall black stone keep rose at the center of the fortress, while grey stone walls obscured the horizon.

A gray-haired, wrinkle-faced man in Tar Ebon livery descended the stairs coming down from the inner keep. "Your Highness, this is a surprise." He saluted before approaching and kissing her offered hand.

"Surprise was our intention, Colonel Fulczyk. Our enemies must not know of our plans."

"You can trust me, Your Highness," the colonel said.

"I thought I could trust my household servants too," the queen mused. "That did not end well."

The colonel chuckled nervously. "A raven brought news of the attack on Tar Ebon. I am sorry for the loss of your son." His eyes drifted to Feodora.

The queen inclined her head. "Thank you. The cult will pay for their attacks."

"Why have you come so far north?" the colonel asked, wringing his hands. His eyes swept over Emma, Kylie and the royal siblings. "Do you desire to go beyond the river?"

"No, Colonel. We are far enough north."

"Will you be staying here for long?"

"No. We won't even be staying the night. I wanted to show the girls the outer walls, then we'll be on our way east toward Seaholme."

Emma furrowed her brows. Why was the queen telling the colonel their true destination Why wouldn't she say it was secret or give him misinformation?

"Seaholme?" the colonel asked. "There's not much there."

"Our business there is our own, Colonel. The wall, please?"

He cleared his throat. "Of course. Right this way." He backed away and headed toward a set of stairs that winded up toward the top of the high northern walls of the fort.

"It's cold," Feodora complained as they walked.

"Wait until we get atop the wall," Emma said. "The north wind will blow right into us."

"How do you know that?" Feodora asked. "Have you been to the Haguesfort before?"

"No," Emma replied. "But I grew up in Ironforge - southeast of here. I know how the north wind can be this close to the tundra."

"How did you stay warm?"

"A vast network of pipes beneath the city carry excess heat from the forges. Every house had a basement with a grate that opened to the pipes and let heat into the house."

"At the palace we use fireplaces to heat the palace."

"Yes, I'm well aware how you heat buildings in Tar Ebon," Emma replied. "I've only lived there for most of a year."

Feodora sniffed but said nothing further.

"All's been quiet, Your Highness," the colonel said as he led the group up the stairs. "The nomadic tribes have kept to themselves throughout the spring. Summer should be quiet as well."

"They normally descend during winter, do they not?" the queen asked.

"Aye, when the Hague River freezes, they cross on foot and in their sleighs."

"Do they steal women and children?" Feodora asked. "Old Nan used to tell us stories of the frost tribes before bed."

The queen tsked. "If I'd known she was telling you such tall tales..." she trailed off and let out a deep sigh. "The frost tribes, or Frigorn People, as they are officially known, are nomads. They come south to trade and find relief from the winter storms."

"Then why do you have a garrison here if they're not a threat?" Feodora pressed.

"Because not all of the Frigorn People are friendly. The Elgeriy tribe are the friendliest, and closest to the river. But other tribes, such as the Bombasi and Riyuki tribes are more war-like."

"Usually the Bombasi and Riyuki tribes are too busy fighting one another to descend south to attack the king...Federation," the colonel put in. "But during the height of winter they will often use the fog that forms above the river to cross and raid the homesteads and villages in this region."

"Oh," Feodora said.

"They were almost wiped out during the Krai'kesh invasion," the queen said. "The Krai'kesh swept down from the north, wrecking this very fort as they came." They had reached the top of the wall by that point. She leaned over and pointed down. "Take a look."

Emma, Kylie and the royal siblings approached the wall and peaked over. She gaped. Massive gashes were gouged in the *stone*. "They could pierce stone?" she asked after straightening.

"Yes," the queen said. "They would have pierced the walls of Tar Ebon too, if not for the magical nature of the black stone."

"Because the molecules are bonded so close," Emma muttered. It made sense - the air between the molecules of stone had been forced out, making the walls harder to pierce.

"What was that?" the colonel asked, frowning.

"Nothing," Emma said, ignoring the raised eyebrow from Feodora. The crown princess did not know about Emma's implant.

Time to change the subject. She pointed toward the white glaciers and slate gray mountains in the distance. "That's quite a sight, isn't it?"

Feodora took the bait and followed Emma's finger. "Yes, if it wasn't so cold it would be beautiful." She shivered dramatically to emphasize the cold.

The north wind was biting, but not that cold. "You could always summon a shield to block the air."

"That would take too much energy," Feodora complained.

Then don't complain about the cold, Emma thought dully.

"The river moves quick up here," Kylie said. Perhaps she was trying to change the subject also?

Emma eyed the river. *Now that would be cold.* She saw no ice on the racing surface but had no doubt she could die of hypothermia in minutes. A shiver made its way up her spine as she remembered a year earlier when she'd almost died from the condition after absorbing her brother's fire spell.

"The Hague River freezes solid for two or three months of the year. But the rest of the time it is like this."

"And that bridge?" Emma asked, pointing to a massive stone bridge. "Has that always been there?"

"Aye, since the days of the Founding. The Krai'kesh could not harm it, for it was built with black stone."

"Why wasn't the Haguesfort built with the same?" she asked.

"The inner keep was," he said, pointing back to the large spire they'd passed on their way to the wall. "But they ran out of magic, or materials, the record isn't clear, and the outer wall was not reinforced with magic."

Emma closed her eyes and reached out with her senses, stretching down into the grey stone at her feet. *I can feel the space,* she thought, sending the air gaps between the molecules of the stone. *I wonder if I could turn it into black stone.*

"Emma," Kylie said in a warning tone. "I know what you're thinking."

"It'll be quick," Emma protested while not releasing her magic. "Trust me." Her friend's reply was lost as she concentrated on the space within the stone. *How do I draw the air out without letting other air in to fill the gap?* She probed and tried to remove molecules of air she found in one small area, but more air rushed in to fill the gap. *It's like water filling the cracks of a stone floor.*

"You're doing it wrong," Feodora's voice cut through the silence of Emma's mind. "You don't remove the air - you draw the stone sections together and it squeezes the air out."

"Oh," Emma said, feeling silly. Of course, that made sense. She released her magic partially and opened her eyes. "Can you show me?"

Feodora sniffed. "I thought you'd never ask. Observe."

Emma's face burned. *She could have been a little humbler about it. But I could have been humbler too.*

Her focus centered on two chunks of stone separated by a narrow ravine of air. Magic tendrils streaked out from Feodora's hands and into the stone. Then, as Emma watched, the chunks of stone glowed in her mind's eye and closed with one another, inch by inch. Within moments, though it might have been hours, time often slowed when casting, the two chunks were like one solid piece of stone. Then, Feodora *pushed* on the stone and the particles that formed its structure collapsed without splitting. The stone beneath their feet shook.

"Are you sure this is safe?" Emma asked, voice trembling. She frowned. How had Kylie become taller than her?

"Look down," Feodora commanded.

Emma did. The two chunks of stone now formed one big square of black stone, several inches below the surrounding grey stone. "What...," she began.

"Stone can be bound together and compressed. When it's compressed, if no new stone is added to the existing mass it shrinks in size."

"Oh," Emma said. It made sense, now that the princess explained it. "Because our magic cannot create matter."

"Correct. We can create energy to a degree, either by drawing it from ourselves, such as body heat, or from the environment, such as the moisture in the air. We can convert mass from one form to another, but not destroy or create it."

Not that we know of, Emma thought. She'd seen some fantastic things in the Halls of Light months earlier when she and Isabelle inadvertently stranded themselves in the technological wonder. *Did the founders have some way to perform such feats?* Isabelle's mother, Bridgette, was known to summon weapons seemingly from thin air, though Isabelle had explained she stored the weapons in the shadow realm and reached into said realm to withdraw them. Still, if matter could be withdrawn from the shadow realm, could energy, and other forms of matter, be siphoned from it as well? *The generator in the basement of the Tower seems to suggest it's possible. But can lowly mages like us do it?* She'd have to ask Isabelle the next time they saw one another.

The queen chuckled. "Now that you've reinforced a tiny portion of the wall - and created a tripping hazard for the colonel's soldiers - I think it is time we make for Seaholme."

The colonel, though he remained quiet, gaped at the sunken stone before shaking his head. "Yes...yes...we will be sorry to see you go of course, but perhaps it is for the best."

He doesn't want us to continue experimenting on his precious garrison, Emma thought. *As if we would seriously damage it.* Images flashed through her imagination of the buildings, black and grey alike, crumbling to the ground, with the three mages at the center. *Okay, maybe we could.*

The queen exchanged a handful of pleasantries with the colonel and then they were on the road, heading east. *What dangers might await us in Seaholme?*

Chapter 12

Two days after departing the Haguesfort, the queen's party reached the outskirts of an unassuming village established a few hundred yards from the edge of the Hague River and on a plateau. *I'm guessing that's to prevent the river from surging and flooding the town,* Emma thought. It was the first settlement they'd seen on their journey east. The road inclined gently as they rode.

"Welcome to Seaholme," the queen called from near the head of their procession. She was not at the immediate front - that honor went to the captain of the guard and the outriders. Her children and Emma and Kylie rode directly behind her while more knights formed the rear-guard.

Seaholme boasted no walls, not even a wooden palisade, and the few villagers going about their business in the mid-afternoon light looked surprised to see armed soldiers riding up the muddy lane that served as the main thoroughfare of the small village.

This *is where we're supposed to be safe from the cultists? This place couldn't save us from a rain storm, let alone a coordinated attack.* Sure, it was on a plateau several hundred feet above river-level, but assailants would simply run up the road and pass inside with ease.

The captain of the guard must have known their ultimate destination, for he led them toward an unassuming wooden manor built on the bluff overlooking the river.

A pair of guards held their hands above their sword hilts but did not draw their blades. "State your business here," one guard called.

"Do you not recognize your queen?" Captain Zomarski challenged.

The two exchanged glances, eyes wide, before moving their hands away from their swords. "Of...of course," one guard said. "Let us announce your presence to the steward."

"That won't be necessary," the queen said, swinging off her horse unaided and striding toward the wooden stairs. She ignored the gaping mouths of the manor guards and approached the thick doors at the top. Only then did she stop.

Captain Zomarski and four guards followed the queen. The captain opened the doors and entered with two guards while the others flanked the queen.

"Should we go up?" Emma asked, in part toward the crown princess and in part to Kylie. *Whoever answers first.*

"Decorum states we wait outside until summoned," Feodora said.

What does she know of decorum? Her brother was the one who would have learned all the decorum, right? "Kylie?"

Her friend shrugged. "It makes sense to me."

"Come along, children," the queen called over her shoulder before entering the dim interior of the manor.

Emma shot Feodora a triumphant glance and smirked before being the first up the stairs.

The inside is as unassuming as the outside, she thought as she passed the threshold. *And it's more like a longhouse than a manor.* A single chandelier with a dozen candles hung from the center of the ceiling, while a half dozen sconces occupied the right and left walls of the building. A fire burned in the hearth at the far end of the manor, obscured by the fanciest piece of furniture in the room - a pair of wooden thrones, both of which sat unoccupied.

Two guards, who stood guard next to a door at the rear of the throne room, looked at one another before one disappeared through the door.

The queen stopped a few dozen feet from the thrones and looked around. "The audience chamber is in need of a good cleaning." She made her point by swiping a finger along the back of a pew and holding it up to inspect. Dust obscured her fingerprint.

Oh, so this is only the audience chamber, Emma thought as she came to stand behind the queen. *The rest of the manor must be behind that door.* That made more sense than the idea that the steward of the queen's secret estate lived in the scarcely furnished throne room.

At last, after the queen and her retinue had been waiting for several minutes, the rear door burst open and a scrawny black-haired man scurried out, wringing his hands. A half dozen servants and as many guards followed. A scraggly-haired blonde woman emerged last.

That must be the steward, Emma thought. *And his wife? She doesn't look terribly well-kept.* Then again, the queen had arrived in the middle of the day, unannounced, giving the steward and his wife little time to prepare.

The steward took his seat in the throne, his wife at his side. He gestured and the servants fanned out with dusters to clean the room or poke the fire. The guards took up positions flanking the thrones.

Why does he need guards when in the presence of his sovereign? Emma thought.

"Your majesty," the steward said in a slick voice that reminded Emma of fish salesmen back in Tar Ebon. "What an...unexpected surprise."

"Leonard Uronska," the queen replied, inclining her head. "We are in need of sanctuary in the catacombs."

The man's eyes widened. "Of...of course, my queen. Let me get them prepared and..."

"There should be nothing to prepare," the queen interrupted. "They have been sealed until this moment. Lead us to them. Time is of the essence, as our enemies could even now be on their way."

"Enemies?" the steward asked, voice quavering, making no move to rise. "You would bring enemies to Seaholme?"

"Have you forgotten, Steward, that this estate belongs to the royal family? We will of course allow the village to come with us into the catacombs. Have your guards bring the villagers to the manor with only the food and drink they can carry."

His eyes darted over the queen's retinue, lingering on Emma, Kylie and the royal family. "You've brought your entire family?"

"Yes. Their lives were threatened in Tar Ebon," the queen said. "We believed they would be safer in the catacombs than in the capital. Now if you'll lead us to them...," she let the words hang, making it clear it was *not* a suggestion.

At that moment, the main doors of the manor burst open and one of the guards the captain's guard had conversed with earlier burst in. "My Lord," the guard began. "Smoke has been sighted to the south, west and east!"

"What?" the steward demanded, eyes widening and standing up. "Is this your doing?" he demanded, pointing a finger at the queen.

"Watch your tone to your queen," Captain Zomarski warned.

"I warned you our enemies may be close behind us. Time is of the essence, Steward. Lead us to the catacombs and evacuate the village into them."

"But what of the other villages?" he asked. "You would abandon them to their fate?"

Why is he stalling? Emma thought. *Do as your queen commands.*

The queen sighed, caught in a conundrum. "I will lend some of my guards to bolster your own in the field."

"And your mages?" he asked, pointing toward Emma.

How did he know we were mages? Something didn't feel right.

The queen looked back toward Emma and the others. "Emma, Kylie, would you accompany my guards to help shepherd the other villages here to the catacombs?"

"I want to go as well," Feodora protested.

"No, you are the crown princess," the queen began. "It's too dangerous."

"They could need my help!" she shouted.

"My answer is final," the queen said coolly. "Now, show us the catacombs," she commanded.

"Of course," the steward replied, gesturing to the rear door. "Right this way."

"Emma and Kylie, you will go with Captain Zomarski and a dozen of my guards west to the first of the villages on fire. Help extinguish the fire and escort the villagers to the outskirts of Seaholme."

Emma nodded and saw Kylie nod out of the corner of her eye. *I'm not comfortable with this, but I'll do it.* "Of course, Your Majesty."

Captain Zomarski seemed ready to argue, for he'd turned to the queen and opened his mouth, but the queen held up a hand and turned to face him. "Captain, I'll be fine. The shelter is nigh impenetrable."

"Yes, my queen, but..." he looked sideways at Steward Uronska. "I will trust your judgment."

The queen offered a wry smile and inclined her head. "Go in grace and be safe."

The captain turned and called out the names of a dozen knights, then pointed to Emma and Kylie. "You two with me."

She'd already told us that, Emma thought, but did not argue. She looked to Feodora and considered saying farewell, but the princess stared straight ahead. *Goodbye to you too, princess,* she thought before turning and following the captain.

Outside, their horses still waited, held by stable boys who had not been there when they entered the manor.

A dozen guards wearing the livery of the steward sat atop their horses. They glared at the queen's guards but said nothing.

Not very friendly, are they? Emma thought. *Perhaps they're jealous of how well-dressed the queen's guards are.* The steward's guards, wearing only a metal breastplate and boiled leather armor everywhere else, stood in stark contrast to the chain and plate mail worn by the queen's guards.

Chapter 13

Emma estimated an hour had passed before they arrived at the first village. Their guide, the captain of the steward's guards, Captain Andola, had identified the village as Woodhaerst.

Oh boy, Emma thought as she saw the billows of smoke rising from several buildings. The whole town seemed to be on fire. Villagers ran here and there, women shepherding children along or bringing up buckets of water from the well while the men ran the buckets to various buildings and tossed the water on them or at some flame inside. No cultists were in sight.

"Spread out," Captain Zomarski ordered, pointing. "Help the villagers to safety and line them up out here. We'll escort them back to Seaholme."

The queen's knights and steward's guards spread out, obeying his orders.

The captain then snapped and pointed to Emma and Kylie. "You two, can you make yourself useful and do something about those fires?"

"That's what we're here for," Emma said testily. She looked toward Kylie. "Spread out, or stay together?"

"Spread out," Kylie suggested. "It's just fire. It should be easy to disperse."

"Yeah," Emma agreed. There wasn't enough water around for them to throw toward the fire, and the air did have a chill in it, meaning it would be easier to disperse the heat into the air than it would in, say, the deserts of Shar'hai.

She and her friend spread out, Kylie taking one side of the village, Emma taking the other side.

At the first building, a general store, by the look of it, Emma closed her eyes and studied the building, and the source of the smoke, with her mind. The heat caused by the flames licking at the wood that made up the general store was small right now but steadily growing. Pools of water littered the wood floor, showing the efforts by the villagers to save their town. Only those pools of water had stopped the building from being burned to ash before Emma and her party arrived.

Okay, focus on getting the heat out, Emma thought. *Then extinguish the flame.* She reached out with her magic and touched the hotspot. She formed a funnel above the heat and felt the red-orange glow spreading up the funnel instead of continuing outward. The wood the funnel touched started absorbing the heat and burning, creating an impromptu chimney, but she reasoned it was better to burn up than out. After several seconds, the top of the air funnel had poked into the open air and the heat was exhausting and fading into the cool northern wind.

Now to focus on the fire itself, she thought. Fire needed air, oxygen, to be precise, to thrive. Deprive it of oxygen and it would cease burning. This part was trickier for a first-year student. *I can do it, though.* She canceled the funnel and instead focused on containing the fire in a ball of air. Then she hardened the barrier of air by compressing its molecules so that it became as solid as a brick wall.

Now to wait, she thought. Moment-by-moment the fire shrank as it consumed what little oxygen remained in the bubble of air. At last the fire blinked out of existence.

Letting out a breath, she looked around. The guards had begun lining the survivors up, men, women and children clutching their meager possessions. One house had erupted into full flame, while Kylie had seemingly extinguished the flame from the building she'd gone to.

"My baby is in there!" a woman shrieked from a building over. She pointed frantically to the fully engulfed house. Men ran with buckets, but Emma knew they would be too late.

Closing her eyes again, Emma pushed through the pounding in her head and stretched her magic out toward the engulfed house. *There, a person*, she thought, identifying the "baby" the woman referred to, stuck in a room at the far corner of the two-story home on the second floor. The flames continued their relentless advance.

I can't contain all that flame, she thought. *And I can't drain the air out without suffocating the child. But I could make a hole in the building for the kid to jump out.* She focused on the wood at the child's back. Then she summoned a razor-thin line of air and formed it into a circle. She set it rotating and pressed the spinning circle against the wood. As if the air were a saw, it sent sawdust flying in every direction. Within moments Emma felt the resistance to the air-saw disappear and released the spell - she was through.

Now how do I pull the plug out *instead of inward?* She didn't want to crush the child. She summoned air and formed a type of cup over the circular piece of wood she'd cut around. Then she removed the air, creating an area of low pressure. Slowly, the wooden circle pulled toward her. *Just a little more.* Moments later the circle fell outward, and she released her spell. It crashed to the ground and dust billowed into the air.

Emma released her magic. "Jump through!" she shouted toward the child, a boy, she now saw, who now peaked out from the hole, eyes wide with terror.

The mother of the child joined the chorus, pleading for her son to jump.

The boy looked over his shoulder, then back. "I'm scared!" he shouted.

"If you don't jump, you'll die!" Emma shouted back, desperate for the boy to hear reason. "I'll catch you!" she suited action to word and stepped atop the wood cut-out, arms stretched upward.

At last, the boy stepped forward and then, with a little jump, was airborne. He fell and landed in Emma's arms.

"I've got you," Emma reassured him before rushing over to his mother.

The flames, as though encouraged by the fearful retreat of the child, surged onward to consume the room the boy had occupied moments earlier.

"Thank you, thank you, thank you!" the woman said between sobs as she embraced her boy.

"My pleasure," Emma said.

By now, two more houses lay in burnt ruins. Kylie fought the fire on another house.

Emma jogged over to her friend. "Do you need help?"

"No," Kylie responded, voice distant. "I've got it."

Emma considered starting on another building, but it looked like all the villagers had assembled, the fire-fighting efforts had ceased, and the guards were preparing to move out.

Kylie finished moments later and swiped sweat from her brow. "We did what we could," she replied. "They'll rebuild the rest."

"I guess," Emma thought. "Why would the cultists attack all these towns?"

Kylie shrugged. "Do the cultists need a reason?"

"To destroy resources? Yes."

"Maybe they took what they wanted and burned the rest."

"Let's find out," Emma replied. She approached the mother clutching her son as they made their way to the assembled crowd. "Excuse me?"

"Oh. Yes?" the woman asked, turning to her.

"Did the Cult of Rae come through here? Are they the ones who did this?"

"Yes," she said. "They took our young girls and rode off with them but set fire to the village before they did."

Emma clutched her stomach, suddenly feeling ill. "Girls?"

"Your age," the woman amended. "You can guess what will happen to them."

"Yes, I can," Emma said. *Rape.* She clenched her hands into fists. "Which way did they go? No, wait, east is my guess."

"Yes, they marched them east. I heard them talk of a ship to the northeast." A tear slid down her cheek. "They took my Marcie."

Northeast. That would put them just past Seaholme. Her stomach sunk. "We will do everything in our power to free her," Emma said. "I promise."

The woman nodded through the deluge of tears but did not speak.

Maybe she realizes that what I'm promising may be outside my power to fulfill. "We have to tell the captain," she said to Kylie.

Together the girls made their way to their horses and rode up to Captain Zomarski. "Captain, may we have a word?"

The captain spared a glance for them. "What is it, mage?"

Emma bristled at being spoken to by her title - a title she hadn't even officially earned yet - but tried to shrug it off. "We have important information." She pressed on before he could interrupt. "The Cult of Rae *did* come through here, and they took several teenage girls with them and set the fires. They're heading northeast."

"I see." His eyes swept the crowd of villagers and then the steward's guards before focusing again on Emma. "Are you sure of this?"

"The woman had no reason to lie. And I rescued her son."

"So the cultists are recruiting by force," he muttered. "Spoils of war and brood mares."

Emma felt her cheeks warm at the idea of the girls being referred to as brood mares but forced herself to respond. "It appears that way, sir."

"Alright. We will continue east as planned and then head northeast to look for these ships. But if Seaholme comes under attack, we return at once." He was not asking for her approval of the plan.

"I understand," Emma offered anyway.

"And speak no word of this to the steward's guards. I don't trust them."

Founders, I wonder why? Emma thought sarcastically. The steward had appeared to be a sleaze-ball from the moment she laid eyes on him. She wouldn't put it past him to backstab the queen. *So then why are we out here instead of back at Seaholme?* "As you wish," she said.

Minutes later, the refugees were set on a path toward Seaholme - though it would likely take them several hours to reach the seaside town - with two guards as escort, while the remaining forces headed east toward where more smoke rose.

THE SECOND TOWN THEY came to, Swinford, sat along the banks of a river and boasted a ford across said river, hence its name.

Swinford looked to be in much worse shape, for more buildings were reduced to ashes, more were on fire and there seemed to be fewer villagers combating the fires.

"Same procedure here!" Captain Zomarski ordered. The guards spread out as they had before, calling out to the villagers and looking for survivors among the burning wreckage.

Emma closed her eyes and stretched her mind toward a nearby house. *No life here*, she thought. Humans stood out distinctively from elements, structures or other inanimate things to the perception of a mage. She released her magic and looked around.

Again, no teenage girls were in sight. *The cultists hit here too.*

The steward's guards hung back at this village, not lending aid and remaining mounted as the queen's guards took on the task of marshalling the ragged villagers.

What are they waiting for? Emma thought. She opened her mouth, intending to call out to them and inquire as to why they weren't offering aid, when she sensed a powerful spell gathering in the east. "Magic!"

she shouted, drawing upon her own magic and feeling Kylie summon
hers.

A large fireball streaked out of the woods to the east, heading toward the mounted knights belonging to the queen. It split as it went,
one ball becoming a dozen smaller balls, reminding Emma of the time
she'd seen a comet split into pieces as it shot across the night sky as a
child.

Emma summoned a wall of air and cast it onto the path of the oncoming flame barrage. The fire balls slammed against the wall of air and
she gritted her teeth as she strained to hold the invisible barrier against
impact. It held, with only the ground being scorched.

I'm not going to play this game. Time to go on offense from the start.
She walked toward the forest, swirling air around herself and readying a
cyclone spell. *Obscure their view with leaves*, she thought as she cast the
cyclone forward. The wind flung leaves into the air, obscuring her view
of the forest as the cyclone disintegrated. The enemy mage still blazed
like a beacon as she closed her eyes and opened her mind's eye.

Firestorm, she thought, sending a stream of flames toward the cloud
of twirling leaves. The leaves caught fire and soon the trees had caught
fire and human screams of agony drifted on the wind as she burned any
left in the forest alive. A surge of magic suggested the enemy mage protecting himself.

After several moments, as the ashes from the scorched leaves drifted
down to cover the burnt corpses of her enemies, Emma stalked through
the ruins of the burnt forest toward the flickering beacon that was the
enemy mage. She found him sitting against an oak tree, burnt hand
clutching his side.

The enemy mage attempted to draw upon his magic. It flickered for
a moment around him before disappearing.

He's too weak from the attack, Emma realized. *In defending himself,
along with the first fire attack on us, he depleted his energy too much.* A
feral grin formed on her face as she conjured lightning. She thrust out

her hand and streaks of white lightning arced out to form a connection between her and the wounded mage, who spasmed uncontrollably before falling over, head lolling unnaturally. The magic flare in her mind blinked out. But she sensed more magic behind her.

Turning, Emma raced back the way she'd come. She stopped in her tracks when she saw mounted men fighting one another. *The queen's men and the steward's guards?* Emma thought. *Fighting one another?*

The source of the magic she'd felt made itself clear - Kylie stood facing off against two guards, while a third lay on the ground clutching at his eyes. Even as Emma watched, a guard lunged with his sword and Kylie blocked it with a lasso of air.

She's not strong enough. Emma had much more magical endurance than her friend, who was one of the weakest mages at the Tower. Pushing through her own exhaustion, Emma drew upon what felt like the last of her reserves and readied a spell to help Kylie. A pair of fireballs, which she hoped her friend would sense and duck beneath, arced toward the guards.

Kylie ducked and the fireballs caught the two men in the chest, sending them flying backward. She turned to Emma and waved.

Emma nodded before sprinting up to the girl. "What the hell is going on?" she asked.

"The steward's men - they were waiting to ambush the queen's guards. As soon as you disrupted those fire balls they struck. Took down two queens' men before Captain Zomarski rallied his men."

"Bloody hell," Emma swore. "At least our side is winning," she said.

Indeed, Captain Zomarski and half a dozen of his men faced off against four mounted guards belonging to the steward. Said foes swiveled their heads this way and that, looking for a way out or an advantage, Emma wasn't sure.

"Surrender and you will not be harmed," Captain Zomarski shouted.

One of the four, Captain Andola, spat. "We'll die before we surrender to the likes of you!"

Captain Zomarski shook his head. "That can be arranged. Do the three of you wish to say differently? Or are you committed to dying too?"

The three guards sitting a few feet behind their captain looked to one another, then sheathed their swords. "Sorry, we didn't sign up for this," the first guard said.

"Traitors," Captain Andola hissed, rounding on them.

Captain Zomarski kicked his horse into action. It surged forward and smacked him in the side of the head with the flat of his blade. Their foe toppled to the ground and lay still, though his chest still inflated and deflated.

"Disarm these three," he said, pointing at the remaining three guards. "Then clap them all in irons. I want answers." He looked around and spotted Emma, then beckoned to her.

Emma rode over to the man. "They betrayed you," she observed lamely.

"Yes. As soon as you left the enemy attack began, they struck. If you hadn't annihilated their reinforcements waiting in the woods, we would have been overrun and possibly beaten."

"Why would the steward betray us?" Emma asked. "What does he have to gain?"

"That's what I aim to find out. But right now we need to return to the queen. She could be in danger. Get these people ready to move out!"

"What about the last village? And the girls?"

"I told you that if Seaholme came under attack I would prioritize them. It *is* being attacked - only from within."

Emma nodded, frustrated for the poor girls who were taken having to wait even longer for rescue but accepting it.

"Good. Then mount up and get ready to go."

Chapter 14

The captain had spared no guards for the refugees this time. They'd been put on the path and told to head straight for Seaholme, though Emma wondered how much safer it was than their villages. *Could the steward be working with the Cult of Rae? Or just for himself? He didn't seem happy to see the queen.*

Their party neared the outskirts of town but noticed nothing out of the ordinary until the steward's manor came into sight.

Captain Zomarski reigned up, waving the others back before they were seen. "There are dozens of soldiers waiting out in front."

"All the steward's men?" Emma asked. "Does he have that many?"

Captain Zomarski shook his head. "I didn't get a good look at them, but it looks like only a few serve the steward. The rest looked to be dressed like the brigands you fought on the road north."

"So they are working with cultists," Emma concluded.

The captain glared back to where Captain Andola sat bound to a horse, still unconscious.

Is he wondering whether he still needs him alive? It was clear the cultists were behind this. But perhaps he could still be of use in telling them *why* the steward chose to betray them.

"What's the plan?" Kylie asked. She'd been quiet on the ride back to town, with bags under her eyes and slumped in her saddle. It would surprise Emma if she even had a single spell in her until she got food and rest.

"I don't know," Emma said. Her own reserves of magic were quite low, Kylie's were near-depleted, so they would be of little help. "Where is the queen?" she wondered aloud.

Captain Zomarski turned his glare on her. "Let us hope they made it to the catacombs safely."

A bird tweeted in the distance, then a second, closer, and a third, then a fourth.

Those birds are louder than usual, Emma thought. She looked up but saw no birds on any of the rooftops. *So if there aren't any birds around to tweet...what's making that noise?* She stepped forward and looked around the corner.

Her answer came a moment later when, from atop the building to their right and left arced several dozen arrows. The sharp points struck several of the soldiers and guards waiting in front of the manor. A second volley, more from the north and south, flew and struck those who'd survived the first wave.

Emma tried to get a glimpse of who was attacking, but right then another sight caught her eye.

A dozen riders wearing dark brown cloaks with the hoods up thundered into the open square in front of the remaining foes. They held short bows, with arrows nocked, and released a third wave. Then, the first group of archers launched a volley, followed immediately by the second group.

By now, those enemies who had not retreated into the building were dead in the dirt at the bottom of the stairs. Which, by Emma's estimate, was most of them.

The newcomers stowed their short bows and then the lead rider threw back his hood, revealing short brown hair. He cast a glance in Emma's direction.

Emma gasped and put her hand over her mouth. "Dawyn," she said aloud. He and his rangers had come.

Without giving the remaining enemies any time to prepare, Dawyn kicked his enormous black stallion into motion and charged, drawing his sword as he went. He swung and struck the first of the guards foolish enough to stand against him, cutting them down. His horse reared and knocked the blade out of another guard's hand before crushing them with his hooves. The other three guards fled up the stairs into the manor.

The captain, who had moved his horse up beside Emma's sometime during the chaos, waved his men forward. "There's one of the few men in the Federation we know won't betray us."

Dawyn turned his horse and watched Emma and her group approach. "Greetings," he said solemnly, inclining his head.

"Supreme Commander," Captain Zomarski said, also inclining his head in greeting. "I am pleasantly surprised to see you here."

"How did you get up here?" Emma blurted. "I mean, up here so fast. Weren't you in Tar Ebon?"

"I think what she means to say is, she's grateful you showed upon when you did, but wants to know what drove you to head north," Kylie chimed in.

Dawyn smiled at Emma's abrupt questions. "Our intelligence showed mass movements of cultists headed north. The queen went ahead with her troops because she was concerned about her children's well-being, and I followed days later with my Rangers when it became clear the cult had a target in mind."

"Seaholme?" Emma guessed.

He nodded. "We don't know why, but intelligence we were able to gather told of the cultists gathering up teenage girls, and some boys, from towns and villages across the regions north and east of Tar Ebon and ushering them north. That, coupled with what lies beneath our feet, could mean the Cult of Rae knows something we don't."

"Ethan and Richard went east," Emma said. "Have you received word of them?"

Dawyn shook his head. "We reached the farm belonging to Richard's family but found signs of a struggle and magical devastation. But no sign of the boys, and those locals who survived said they were among those sent north."

"No," Emma whispered, aghast.

"Are more rangers waiting in the woods?" Captain Zomarski asked.

"I brought one hundred rangers with me - a large portion of our available force of rangers. Most are on these rooftops or behind you, but a few groups are working to locate the main enemy camp."

"From what we heard, they were going to load the teenagers on a ship northeast of here," Emma said. "That could be their base."

"I will have my scouts focus on that direction."

Captain Zomarski spoke. "With respect, Supreme Commander, will one hundred rangers be able to stand up against what may well be an army? Up to this point we have engaged what amounts to raiding parties, but what if their main force is being held in reserve?"

Dawyn nodded. "I thought the same. That is why, before I left, I sent word to Bridgette in the hopes that she can return to Tar Ebon and shift the army north. Based upon where we presume she was in her travels and her speed to return, plus the time to muster the remnants of the army, they should be here soon." He looked over the gathered queens' guards. "Where is the queen?"

"She sent us to help with several villages that were on fire," Captain Zomarski began. "She was going to the catacombs with an escort of guards and her family."

Dawyn adopted a grim expression. "This bodes ill. If they've reached the chamber..." he stopped. "We must get inside at once."

"My men and I are always ready," the captain said. "Though we have prisoners who should be overseen."

"I'll leave two rangers behind to watch them. And the rangers on the rooftop will form a perimeter around the town." He turned his gaze to Emma and flicked to Kylie a moment later. "Can the two of you use your magic?"

Emma shook her head. "Not well, sir. We've nearly exhausted our stores of magic during the last few hours and need time to eat and drink to restore our strength." She straightened as best she could. "But we will gladly fight until our stores are fully depleted."

"A noble gesture," he said. "And we may need every last ounce of your strength. Let's go." Without further preamble, he dismounted and stormed up the steps.

Emma shared a worried look with Kylie, then hurried to dismount. Could mages burn out? Stop being able to channel magic? She'd heard stories that suggested it was possible. *We might find out today.*

"Stay near the back," Captain Zomarski ordered, pointing at Emma and Kylie. "Let the soldiers go first."

You'll get no argument from me, Emma thought. "Yes, sir," was all she said.

Dawyn opened one side of the door while a ranger opened the other. The remainder of the armed men waited further down the stairs, in case arrows or bolts came flying through the opening. But when no ambush came, Dawyn looked around the corner and waved the soldiers forward. "It's clear."

The throne room looked much as it had when they'd departed, except the fire in the hearth had died out. *Were the servants sent home? Or imprisoned? Or worse?* Emma thought.

"This does not bode well," Dawyn said as he strode toward the rear door. "It means they've likely breached the catacombs and have fortified themselves."

And what of the royal family? Emma wanted to ask.

Once through the rear door, they found a series of hallways and a stairwell leading to a second floor. The rangers drew their bows and aimed arrows toward the landing in case they were ambushed, but Dawyn ignored the upstairs and instead strode with purpose into the heart of the manor. He took a right and they found themselves in a religious sanctuary of some sort. Symbols Emma didn't recognize hung on the walls. And there sat a stone slab over what looked to be an altar.

Dawyn pulled a sconce out of the wall and twisted it. Then he walked to the other side of the room and did the same to that sconce. A click, followed by a grinding sound, followed as the altar slid to one side.

Emma felt her eyebrows raise. *A secret passage? They did say catacombs, but I didn't think it had a secret entrance.*

This time, an attack came in the form of glass bottle with a flaming cloth hanging from one end flying out and smashing on the stone floor. The pale liquid ignited into red-orange flame.

"Can you extinguish it?" Dawyn called, eyes on Emma.

Emma nodded. "Yes, I can." *I hope.* Closing her eyes, she stretched out with her magic and saw the flame glowing in her mind's eye. It felt different from when material like wood burned. Stronger, somehow. Hotter. *If I can't cool it down, maybe I can redirect the heat.* "Everyone stay back!" she managed to shout. She siphoned the heat from flames and condensed it into a ball of super-heated air above. More heat appeared as the substance burned itself up, and she collected that too. The substance was gone and only a ball of heat, looking like a globe of white when she opened her eyes briefly, remained. She cast it down into the hole from where the bottles came and *unleashed* the heat.

A dozen or more screams erupted, then were silenced as acrid smoke that smelled of human flesh rose through the hole. Emma covered her face with her tunic in a futile attempt to block the smell, while her stomach roiled. Yes, this was war and she'd killed more in the past, but never in this gruesome of a manner. *They must have been roasted alive.*

I conjecture that the heat you condensed reached twelve-hundred degrees Kelvin. Enough to sear their lungs in an instant so that they die of suffocation and...

Okay, okay, I get it, Shadow, Emma thought hurriedly, trying to cut off her AI. *I killed them in a brutal manner.*

On the contrary. It was an efficient manner. You used the heat they generated with their explosives to burn them instead.

Let's agree to disagree. Sometimes the matter-of-fact nature of her implant disturbed her. She put a hand on the side of her head as a massive headache formed. *I can't take much more of this.*

Dawyn whistled. "That's one way to extinguish the flames."

"I'm sorry," Emma apologized, turning to the supreme commander. His brows furrowed. "For what?"

Emma gestured to the hole in the floor. "For that."

"This is war, Emma," he said, voice stern. "We do what we have to do to survive. Do you understand?"

Emma averted her eyes and bowed her head. "I think so."

"Good. Now, it's time to do whatever we must to stop the Cult of Rae. There's no time for reservations." Without waiting for further response, he drew his dual swords and descended the stairs. The others followed.

"You okay?" Kylie asked as she passed, stopping to stand beside her friend.

"Yes," Emma said in a small voice. "Was he berating me for not being brutal enough?"

"I think he just wants you to remain focused. If you freeze at the wrong moment, people could die."

That makes sense, Emma thought. *He could have just said that, though, instead of humiliating me in front of everyone.* She followed them down the stairs, Kylie behind.

"Turn to the right, when you get to the bottom," Dawyn's voice drifted up. "There are bodies to the left."

Emma gaped as she stepped off the bottom step and turned to the right. *It's like a whole new world.* The dull stone of the world above had been replaced by a shining white material. Emma reached out to a wall and felt heat. She knocked and the wall reverberated. *Metal.*

Don't look back, don't look back. The urge to look over her shoulder, at the presumed carnage she had caused, surged within her, but she pushed it down like she might bile when nauseous. It was bad enough there were black streaks along a portion of the wall. Pushing her shoulders back, she followed the others down the right fork.

She ran her fingers along the wall as she walked and slowly the heat faded, and her arm shivered at the cool metal. "So the catacombs aren't really catacombs, are they?" she asked.

"No. This is a piece of an ark ship that belonged to the Founders. The ancient records say that when the ark ship that founded Tar Ebon fell to earth this piece broke off and landed here. Unable to move it, and unable to dismantle it safely, they buried it beneath a mound of dirt and placed this manor above it. Since that day, it has been in the care of the kings of Tar Ebon through their stewards."

"Safely?" Emma asked, latching on to one portion of his response. "What is it?"

"I don't claim to know as much about science as Jason, but from what I understand, it was a piece of the shadow engine that allowed them to travel vast distances rapidly."

"Similar to what was beneath the Tower?" Emma asked.

"I think it was a twin of that, or something," he said, shrugging as he strode down the hall. "I admit I didn't pay as much attention as I should have to his explanation. Now shh, we're nearing the control room, or sanctuary, as it was referred to by the royal family."

The group fell silent, with the rangers and knights drawing weapons as they went. Over twenty people, by Emma's count. *I hope we're enough.* Her head pounded more painfully, as though mocking her. The Founders only knew what they would find ahead of them.

They reached a metal door with writing upon it indicating "authorized personnel only" and "danger - hazardous material warning" among others. *And we're walking right into it.*

Dawyn stepped to one side of the door, near a rectangular place that reminded Emma of similar features in the Tower. He sheathed both swords. "Once I put my hand on this plate, it will slide to the side. I *do* expect some form of resistance, and it is likely they are holding the royal family hostage. We must do everything in our power to not harm them."

Assuming they're still alive, Emma thought darkly.

"On three." He lifted a hand and counted down from three with his fingers. At zero, he formed a fist and, with his other hand, slapped the plate. A light beamed out, scanning his hand, and then lit green. The door slid up. He drew his blades and passed inside.

As the others stormed in, Emma heard a hollow clattering sound from within. When she passed the threshold, she found a pile of arrow shafts lying on the floor in front of the supreme commander. Then she lifted her eyes and gasped.

The queen and her children sat bound and gagged along one wall of what looked to be a control chamber. Feodora wore a silver Shara'han collar and bruises covered her face, while the queen's head hung down and she looked to be unconscious. Feodora's siblings appeared to be unharmed but quivered where they sat, though their eyes widened when they saw Emma and the others enter.

Opposite the door was a set of controls similar to what she'd seen before in the Halls of Light. Beyond the controls was a panel of windows separating the control room from the chamber beyond, where a pair of pylons formed an upside-down U. A bracket in the center sat empty and the pylons sat immobile.

There was no sign of the royal guards, though there were pools of blood on the floor. *Signs of a struggle?*

The immediate threat came from a dozen soldiers holding bows with arrows nocked and aiming toward Dawyn and his party. Behind them stood perhaps two dozen other men with swords and shields ready.

I knew we should have brought more men, Emma thought.

Dawyn's rangers sheathed their swords and readied their bows and arrows, while Captain Zomarski and his men drew swords and braced to charge or counter-charge.

"Lower your weapons and surrender and you may yet live," Dawyn said.

"Take another step, and the royals get their throats slit," a hulking man near the rear of the enemy formation said.

"Where is Steward Uronska?" Emma demanded. Though she suspected the truth, she had to ask.

"He's gone to meet our master and reap his reward," the man replied.

"Reward for handing you the royal family?"

"No," Dawyn said. "For baiting the royal family to open the door to this chamber and then taking that," he pointed to the empty bracket suspended between the pylons. "The shadow core."

"What would they need that for?" Emma asked.

"I can think of only one thing. To bring Valdorf into this world."

A chill raced down Emma's spine and she shivered. She'd briefly met Valdorf in the shadow realm the year before. But Bridgette had explained that he was locked in the shadow realm, with no way back. "How..."

"Enough talk," the hulking man said. "You fell right into our trap."

"You're the ones who are backed into a corner," Dawyn pointed out.

"Yes, about that," a raspy voice came from a door to the right of the cultist formation. Five men wearing black cloaks emerged. "All part of the plan. We will kill you, Eternal, then take the girls for our master." Magic surged around all five and the magic of the other four streamed into the speaker.

Shit, Emma thought. *So that's how they took Feodora out.* Five mages would have negated her powers completely, allowing them to place the collar around her neck to suppress her ability to reach her magic.

The lead mage started conjuring a spell, flows of magic combining to form a swimming ball of fire. "Now prepare to burn."

"Emma," Dawyn said over his shoulder. "Now's the time to do something if you're able."

Emma wanted to scream that she couldn't do anything, that she was tired and felt on the verge of collapse and her head pounded. She wanted to shout that if she used more magic she could burn herself out. But she also knew that if she admitted defeat her enemies would succeed - they would kill her allies. She nodded. *I can do this. We can do this.* "Kylie, lend your magic to me."

The other girl opened her mouth, probably to offer an identical protestation that Emma had been contemplating, but snapped her mouth shut and nodded. Then she drew upon her magic and extended it to Emma.

Emma seized it and felt a relative trickle of power flooding her body. Still, compared to the drops remaining in her own reserves, it was a stream. *It's something,* she thought. *And if I draw too much we* both *could burn out.*

Now how to stop five mages? They were likely to be fully powered up, to a point where even one could stop both mages combined. Five would have them shackled like Feodora.

Just distract them for a moment, a voice came in her head.

Emma started. It wasn't her inner monologue, and it didn't *sound* like Shadow. It had more of a regal accent. *Who is this?*

Dawyn.

Emma resisted the urge to gape. *But...how...* How had he connected to her? How had he known she had an implant? Had Bridgette said something? Perhaps Alivia?

How I know is unimportant right now, he cut it, conveying a sense of impatience. *Distract them and I will take care of the rest.*

How...

You will see, he snapped. *If you ever wish to be a soldier, learn to obey orders.*

Yes, sir, Emma replied, feeling more abashed than angry. *I'll try lightning.*

Can you create a cloud instead?

I've never...

A cloud is merely condensed moisture. Think like fog. Fog is created due to the rapid change in temperature.

So if I...cooled the air...

It could create fog, yes. Cool it without dehumidifying - without removing the moisture.

I think I can do that.

Good. Emma got the sense that the link closed.

Rapid cooling. She expanded her mind and felt the air in front of her. It felt warm - with a slight current coming out from a vent along the wall. *Where to send the warm air?* An image flared in her mind - of a ring of fire formed by Ethan hurtling toward her a year earlier. *Fire.*

She closed her eyes and extended her arms and spread her fingers, then focused on pulling the heat energy from the air. It streamed toward her and wrapped around her arms, like it once had before. But this time, instead of internalizing the heat, she expelled it into a ball of heat between her spread hands.

The air ignited, forming an orange flame that fed upon the heat she poured into it.

More heat, she thought, opening her eyes incrementally but seeing no fog. She sucked more heat energy toward her, being careful not to attract the moisture molecules she saw in that area. Finally, after the ball of flame had grown to cover almost the entire space between her now-wide arms, she saw an effect, as the moisture molecules slowed their rapid undulation. *Almost there.* One final pull and the moisture slowed to a halt.

She released her hold on the heat in that area, while still maintaining a ball of fire and the room temperature air flooded in again, but this time fog formed.

Now, she thought, though she knew the supreme commander could not hear her in that moment.

The supreme commander, having eyes, drew his swords. Then he *blurred* and appeared *behind* the enemy mages. Emma strained to make him out through the light fog. He swung both blades in backward slashes, instantly beheading two foes, then twisted his wrists and brought the blades back together, decapitating the third enemy.

By the time the other two reacted to their brethren falling, it was too late - they each got a blade through the back, with the points poking through below each mage's rib. He slid them out and wiped the blood off on the cloak of one mage.

In the shocked silence that followed, Dawyn's rangers released their arrows, which streaked through the fog, leaving tiny trails of clear space, striking a dozen of their enemy's compatriots. Then the queen's knights rushed forward into the chaos, slamming into the enemy with ferocious fury.

They're likely upset by the capture of their liege. She looked to Kylie, who looked about to fall over. *Oh, her magic.* She released the hold she had on Kylie's magic, hoping what little she relinquished to her would help. No sooner had the magic left than her headache returned, like horses pounding in her brain.

One enemy tried running toward the royal family, but Dawyn blurred again and stood between him and them. He parried the surprised strike from his foe with one blade, then stuck with the second, stabbing him in the gut.

Within moments, the fight was over and every cultist in the room was dead - all except one. The hulking man who had spoken upon their entering the room bled from a wound in his side, but even then was having his hands and feet bound while another ranger attended to his side wound.

It's over, Emma thought, focusing on where Feodora and her family were being released from their bonds and Feodora from the collar inhibiting her power.

Emma closed her eyes, exhaustion swarming over her and finally dragging her down into sweet unconsciousness.

Chapter 15

"Emma," a disembodied voice said.

Emma groaned.

"Emma?" the voice game again. Female. Kylie? No, Feodora.

Emma opened her eyes slowly and blinked several times as the crown princess came into focus. "Did you have to wake me up?" Emma asked, then coughed due to the dryness of her throat.

"Water?" Feodora asked, offering a mug to her.

She took it, grateful to have the cool liquid flow down her throat and spread through her abdomen. Then she looked around. "Where are we?" She looked down and saw bedsheets. She wore a stained white nightgown that felt two sizes too big.

"In the manor," Feodora answered. "Mother reclaimed it after we were freed."

"How long have I...," she let the question hang.

"You almost died, or so the local healer said." She sniffed. "Not that she knows anything about magic. But you've been asleep for three days."

"I thought I was going to die," Emma admitted. She touched her head. "It felt like my head would split open."

"Can you cast?"

Emma closed her eyes and felt for the spark of magic deep within her. It shone in her mind's eye, filling her with artificial warmth that caused her body to shiver. She grinned and opened her eyes. "Yes! I feel it! Just as strong as before." *Perhaps stronger,* she thought, *if I'm being honest. But that could be my mind playing tricks on me after being depleted for so long.*

Feodora grinned in return. "Good. Kylie was able to use hers as well."

"Where is she?"

"Across the hall. She woke up a few hours before you."

"Good." She fell silent, mulling over her next sentence. "Feodora...did they..."

The crown princess's grin evaporated but she shook her head. "No, they didn't hurt us other than rough-handling us into those chairs. And that damned collar. Have you ever worn one of those?"

Emma shook her head. The class on magical obstruction was a third-year class.

"Well, I'd worn one before in class, but not for so long. It feels like a part of you is cut off, severed. I'd never felt so alone in my life - does that make sense?"

"Yes," Emma whispered. "It's how we all felt before coming into our magic."

"Huh, I never thought of it that way," she replied.

"I had my brother, so I didn't notice as much. But once I developed magic, it felt like a part of me was returning."

"I...I want to apologize," Feodora began.

Emma's eyebrows shot up. The crown princess, *apologizing*? "For what?"

"I haven't been the nicest. To you, to Kylie."

No, you haven't, Emma agreed silently. "I understand," she said, instead. "You were under pressure and in a difficult situation. Your life has been in danger since we left Tar Ebon, and you were thrust into the unknown." It didn't excuse her behavior, but Emma couldn't guarantee she wouldn't have acted the same if the circumstances were reversed.

She nodded slowly. "Yes, but it doesn't make it right. Will you forgive me?"

Emma smiled. "I'll be honored to call you my queen...one day."

Feodora broke into a grin. "Let's hope that is many years from now. I have a lot of exploring to do before then."

"You can explore as queen," Emma pointed out.

"Yes, but it's far more restrictive," Feodora waved a hand as if to dismiss the notion. "As a princess, even the crown princess, I can go where I will without the need for a full entourage."

"Let's focus on surviving the Cult of Rae before we start making plans for our tour of the world," Emma said. "Speaking of the cult, I saw their leader was captured. Plus Captain Andola. Do we know anything?"

"Mother, Dawyn and Bridgette are questioning them both," Feodora said. "It's been three days, two since Bridgette arrived with the army, and all they've been able to discern is that the cult has indeed established a foothold to the northwest of here, along the river. They're trying to discern why."

"They were capturing teenagers," Emma pointed out. "I thought it was to...you know," her face warmed, "but maybe it's a different reason."

"Like what?" Feodora asked.

"I've read of blood magic," Emma said, a chill racing down her spine. "Extract energy from the blood of victims to cast spells."

"Blood magic is forbidden," Feodora said by rote. "Where did you even read about it?"

"Arch mage O'Leary granted me access to the restricted sector this year." She shrugged. "I didn't read much more than a brief description - I don't know the mechanics of it."

Feodora eyed her. "Let's keep it that way, and hope the cult is not using blood magic."

Sensing that her friend didn't want to discuss it further, Emma did not continue her train of thought. *Could blood magic summon Valdorf?*

"Do you want to go see Kylie?" Emma asked into the silence.

Feodora perked up. "Do you feel up to walking?"

"This is no time to be laying in a bed." Suiting action to words, she threw off the blanket and swung her legs over the side. When her bare feet touched the floor, she remembered she was only in a nightgown. "Do you mind fetching me some clothes and my shoes?" She wouldn't feel right traipsing around the manor with soldiers likely patrolling.

Feodora smiled. "Of course. Let me fetch a servant." Without waiting for a reply, she bustled out of the room.

Emma sighed. *What are you up to, Valdorf?* And why hadn't she been able to communicate with Ethan? *Shadow? Has there been any communication from Ethan?*

No, Ma'am, Shadow replied at once. *And if I do say so, I am glad you returned to consciousness.*

Why didn't it happen sooner? I was down for three days, Shadow.

Unfortunately, the level of exhaustion you experienced is outside of my logic parameters.

What does that mean?

There was physically nothing wrong with you, Ma'am, but your mind appeared to be so exhausted you fell unconscious. A similar scenario might be caused by a person staying awake for several days without sleep.

Emma nodded. That made sense. *Can you try to contact Ethan again?*

I will endeavor to try again, Ma'am. One moment. Before Emma could blink, he replied. *Unfortunately I am unable to send any communications. The primary node may still be down.*

How was the supreme commander able to communicate with me using his implant, then?

Peer-to-peer networks may be established in close proximity. Each implant possesses a short-range communication capability which uses a different radio than the long-range communication array, which requires a node for routing.

Okay, I didn't understand half of that, but it sounds like we could communication because we were close?

Correct. I calculate the range to be fifty meters or so.

Feodora returned, servant in tow. "You're about my size. These should fit."

The older woman set a bundle of clothes, underclothes and shoes on the edge of Emma's bed.

"I'm surprised you could find any servants," Emma said.

"The steward may have left, but his servants remained behind or fled into the village. They wanted no part in his treachery, it seems."

"He took some of the younger maids, though," the older woman said.

Feodora cleared her throat. "Yes, well, I'm sure my mother and the supreme commander will come up with a plan to rescue them soon."

"How many troops did Bridgette bring," Emma asked as she donned the new clothes, ignoring the impropriety of undressing in front of her friend and a servant. "Did Isabelle come with her?"

"I didn't count, but a few hundred." She hesitated. "And yes, Isabelle came."

"Why didn't you tell me?" Emma screeched as she laced up her boots, eager to see her friend again.

"She...has some bad news. I wanted to wait until you were at least dressed."

"What sort of bad news?" Emma asked, smile dying like embers in a high wind.

"It's best if she tells you in person."

Despite the impatience gnawing at her mind, Emma nodded. "All right. But first I want to see Kylie. She will want to join us, I'm sure."

Feodora nodded, solemn expression on her face. "This way."

They exited the room Emma had awoke in and found themselves in a hall. As Emma had suspected, a pair of guards stood outside her room and outside Kylie's. More guards patrolled the halls as well. *So much security for what's supposed to be a safe house for the royal family.*

Feodora opened the door to Kylie's room. "Kylie? Emma is up, too."

Kylie sat in her own bed in a room almost identical to Emma's. She grinned wide upon seeing Emma. "Oh good, you're awake! I was worried you would be unconscious for longer."

Despite her worry over what Isabelle had to say, Emma smiled at seeing her best friend. Isabelle was a friend too, but she was almost *too* famous. Kylie was just a small-town girl like Emma. "I guess we were both equally tired." She forced a chuckle. "Are you dressed?"

"Yes." She threw off the covers and set upon putting on her boots. "Where are we going first?"

"Well, Feodora said Isabelle is here, but she has some bad news."

It was Kylie's turn to frown. "I knew Isabelle was here, but I didn't know she had bad news."

And I'm not happy she kept it from us, either, Emma thought. She opened her mouth to give Feodora a tongue-lashing about not keeping secrets from friends but closed it a moment later. Feodora was trying to be their friend - she'd genuinely wanted to spare her new friends whatever bad news Isabelle had. *I guess I would probably act the same in her situation,* Emma admitted. "Shall we go see her and find out?" She turned to Feodora. "Where is she?"

Feodora shrugged. "Last I saw, she was in the throne room. This way." She led them through a series of halls, all interspersed with and patrolled by guards wearing the queen's livery, until they arrived in the familiar throne room Emma recalled from their arrival there.

Isabelle stood in the center of the throne room, four guards surrounding her.

Emma gasped. "Isabelle!" She grasped for her magic.

Isabelle turned and her brows furrowed. "What?" She held up the blades in her hands, which, in the dim light, Emma hadn't noticed were wood. She pointed to the guards. "They're just practice blades."

"Oh," Emma said, cheeks heating. "Sorry, I just woke up." *Way to go, idiot. Thinking the queen's guards would attack her. Paranoid much?*

After all the betrayals they'd experienced thus far, it wouldn't have surprised her.

Isabelle smirked and shook her head. "Let's get back to it. Begin!" She assumed a fighting stance.

Three guards hung back as the fourth moved in. He towered over the relatively diminutive figure of Isabelle. He swung his blade sideways at her chest level.

Before the blade made contact, Isabelle faded to her signature black mist. Only this time, she didn't disappear. She appeared translucent, as though the dark mist had been formed into the shape of a person.

The blade sliced through her translucent avatar and, after it had passed completely through, she rematerialized in a heartbeat and stabbed his chest with both wooden blades. "One down," she said with practiced ease. How many times had she practiced that maneuver?

The other three closed in this time, as one.

This time, Isabelle didn't wait for them to reach her. She dematerialized into mist which faded away faster than real mist in a mid-day summer sun. Then, she reappeared behind the first guard and leisurely dragged her blade across his throat. "Two down." The words were barely out of her mouth and she had disappeared again.

The other two, seeing their comrade "fall," came to stand back-to-back, swords raised and eyes scanning their surroundings.

This time, Isabelle appeared *above* them, falling two or three feet onto the shoulders of one guard, then stabbing him in the heart before spinning around and launching herself toward the final guard. Her momentum toppled him forward and she rode him to the floor where she stabbed him in the back. "And done." She rolled off the guard and stood, raising her arms and dropping the wooden swords to the ground. Then she took a bow.

Emma, along with Kylie and a few dozen other guards and onlookers, clapped. Feodora clapped but had a bored expression on her face, like she'd seen it before. *Maybe she has - how many times has Isabelle been practicing this?*

Isabelle swiped a streak of sweat from her brow as she approached Emma. "Tenth sparring match today," she explained.

"And five hundredth in two days," Feodora said dryly. "That's *all* you've been doing."

"We *are* at war," the girl pointed out. "I will need to do that and more if I'm to survive in a real fight. Those boys are taking it easy on me, I know it," she indicated the "boys" with a thumb over her shoulder.

Emma smiled. "Or you're just that good."

"Or you cheat with your shadow magic," Kylie said, also smiling at her friend.

"It's just a different type of magic, that's all," Isabelle said.

"You're lucky you have both that *and* regular magic," Emma said.

Isabelle shrugged. "I guess."

Emma sobered. "So...Feodora said you had something to tell us? Bad news?"

Isabelle's eyes flickered to Feodora for a moment, then back. She frowned. "Yes, I do. Maybe somewhere more...private?" She turned her head from side-to-side to indicate the room as a whole.

"What does it concern?"

"Ethan and Richard."

Emma's breath caught. "Just tell me."

"But..."

"Isabelle. Now." Were they dead? Is that why he hadn't communicated with her, and not a node being down?

"After my mother and I returned to port in Tar Ebon, she asked me to try to find Ethan and Richard. So I shifted and headed east. I found their farm but..."

"But what?"

"Jeez, I can take on four soldiers at once but can't handle giving you bad news?"

"Tell me," Emma said through gritted teeth.

"They weren't there, Emma. The farm showed signs of an attack and...Richard's parents were there, deceased. In fact, the entire area had been raided. I'm sorry." The words had come out in a flurry and she took a deep breath.

Emma cleared her throat. "Okay, so they're not dead. Ethan and Richard. You didn't find a body, did you?"

"No," Isabelle said slowly. "But I also didn't find them. I think they were captured. I tried shifting around to surrounding towns to no avail."

"I've been trying to contact him since right after we left Tar Ebon, but nothing."

"That's not surprising. My father said the transmission tower in Tar Ebon was damaged by the cultists during their attack. It's disabled long-range communication between implants in this region."

Emma frowned. "Tar Ebon has a transmission tower? Where?"

"On top of the Tower. During the attack, while the Tower was mostly empty, saboteurs struck and damaged it. My father says he *might* be able to repair it but isn't sure. He came along with my mother and the troops, so it won't be fixed anytime soon."

"How is Alivia?" Emma asked, trying to avoid thinking of what might have befallen Ethan. *Maybe they never reached the farm or maybe they escaped or...maybe they were captured.* She had to admit their capture was a possibility.

"She was up and around when we left a few days ago. She wanted to come, but my mother insisted she stay behind. The city still needs to be defended, was her logic."

"Have there been more attacks on the city since we left?"

"Guerrilla attacks continue, on a smaller scale. It's the reason why we couldn't bring thousands of troops with us - aside from my mother's capabilities. Most of the army is deployed around Tar Ebon or have been sent east and south to protect the villages and towns there."

Fat lot of good it did Ethan and Richard, Emma thought. "Dawyn thinks the cultists are close to finding a way for Valdorf to return."

"Yes, I heard," Isabelle replied darkly. "My father disagrees that the shadow core is being used for that, but anything's possible I suppose."

"What else could it be for? He's been capturing teenagers and now the shadow core."

"It could be two separate things," Isabelle said. "Blood magic to summon him and the shadow core for something bigger once he's in our world."

"I hadn't thought of that," Emma admitted, sinking feeling in her stomach. "We have to stop him."

"What do you think my mother and uncle and the queen are discussing right this instant? It's a delicate situation, though, with all the hostages they're suspected to be holding."

"Have they gotten any more information out of the prisoners since we last spoke?" Feodora asked.

"No, they're being surprisingly tight-lipped. My mother wants to use more...questionable methods to get them to talk, but Uncle Dawyn forbids it." She made quotation marks with her fingers. "'Honor demands that they be treated humanely.' I agree with my mother - do whatever is necessary to get the information."

"And *my* mother agrees with the supreme commander," Feodora chimed in. "We are only better than the cultists because we have our moral integrity intact. If we resort to torture, we're no better than them."

"You're both...," Emma cut off as an intense high-pitched screech assaulted her mind. "Agh," she bent over, clutching at her head. *Shadow, what is happening?*

We are receiving a transmission. Attempting to dampen the signal strength. The screech dulled and finally disappeared several agonizing seconds later.

Can you play it? She straightened and met the eyes of her friends, who all wore concerned looks. "Did you hear it too?" she asked Isabelle.

Isabelle shook her head.

I have transcoded the signal. It is ready to play.

Do it.

Emma, it's Ethan.

Emma's breath caught. *Ethan?*

The recording paused. *This is a recording, Ma'am,* Shadow cut in.

Oh. Continue.

I..., he hesitated, *I've been captured. I'm safe, for now, but they have me and Richard held somewhere. It's by a river. They told me you'd know where.*

"Northeast," Emma said aloud.

Ummm...they activated some short-range transmitter to let me send this. They told me...they told me if you don't come, along with the crown princess, her sister, Kylie and Isabelle, they'll kill me and Richard. But only you five, or they'll kill us anyway.

Emma stood stunned, mouth agape at what her brother had told her.

I love you, sis. Don't..., the transmission cut off.

Oh Ethan, she thought. *How I wish I had spoken to you. Shadow, is there any way to broadcast back to him?*

No, Ma'am, the transmission was one-way, and the transmitter is no longer active.

Was it coming from the northeast when it was active?

Yes.

Steeling her nerves, she met the concerned gazes of her friends. "I received a message from Ethan." She proceeded to relay the message word-for-word to them.

"We have to tell my mother," Feodora said. "She'll know what to do."

"I can shift in and grab him and Richard, now that I know where they are."

Emma shook her head. "No. If we tell anyone they'll want to go charging in and Ethan and Richard will be killed before we can get to them. Let's try Isabelle's method, I guess. Can you shift the four of us in? I'm not going to risk Salena's life, since she has no magic. And we're not planning on surrendering."

"Like right now?" Isabelle asked. "I was going to go alone."

"You'll want support."

"Shouldn't we tell someone before we go?" Feodora said.

"No. They'll try to stop us," Emma countered. "Can you do it, Isabelle?"

Isabelle sighed. "Yeah, I can."

"If you want to sneak in," Kylie began, "maybe we should go in the night."

Emma sighed. She hated the idea of waiting Founders knew how many hours before nightfall. But Kylie had a point. "Okay, fine, we'll go at nightfall. What time is it, anyway?"

"Almost supper time," Feodora said, and her stomach growled as if on cue.

"Okay, nightfall it is," Emma said.

"Might as well face death on a full stomach," Feodora grumbled.

"Come on, it'll be fine," Isabelle said. "In and out."

Chapter 16

Hours later, as the grandfather clock heralded the midnight hour in the distance, the four girls assembled in Emma's room. Isabelle wore a weapons belt with knives hanging from it and a black scarf around her neck. She wore her iconic black leather armor.

Kylie and Feodora wore the same as they had earlier, and Feodora had found a belt knife, while Kylie wore no weapon.

As for Emma, she too had found a belt knife, though how much use it would be where they were going was questionable. What mattered there would be magic. *Well, magic and stealth,* she thought. *Better to not be seen than to fight our way out.*

"Everyone ready?" Isabelle asked.

"As ready as we're going to be," Kylie said.

"I still don't like this idea," Feodora said. "For the record."

"We don't have a choice," Emma said. "Ethan and Richard's lives are on the line."

"Well, I left a note for my mother to find in the morning, if things don't go as planned. But they will," Feodora said.

"That's the spirit," Isabelle said. "Everyone hold hands." She extended her hands.

"How does your mother transport an entire army, and you still need us to hold hands to transport us?" Feodora asked, grabbing Isabelle's hand. Kylie took Feodora's other hand.

"Be grateful she can transport us at all," Emma said in defense of her other friend as she grabbed Kylie's hand and completed the circle by clasping Isabelle's. "You just got done apologizing for being snobbish. Don't slide backward." She softened the rebuke with a smile.

"Sorry," Feodora said, casting her eyes down.

Isabelle snorted. "That's a sight I thought I'd never see. But in answer to your question, Your Highness, my mother is trying to teach me how to mass transport people without physical contact, but we've started with inanimate objects, then we'll graduate to animals and lastly to humans. She encompasses everyone with her mind somehow, and I've only just started to learn that. Despite my performance earlier today, I'm still a student." Then, without warning, the world shifted to gray and they were in the shadow realm.

"Don't let go," Isabelle warned. "I don't know what will happen if you let go while we're here."

Their surroundings blurred and they found themselves at the base of the steps leading up to the manor. Emma jolted at the sight of two guards standing at attention behind them in the light gray omnipresent light of the shadow realm. "Can they...see us?"

"No. They can't see or feel us," Isabelle said. "And they only appear in the shadow realm when we're near them. Go a few dozen feet away and they disappear."

"Oh," Emma said, relaxing a little.

"Sorry," Isabelle said, "if the surroundings are unfamiliar after this. I have to make multiple little shifts."

"Like frogs leaping between lily-pads," Kylie said.

"Yes. Just like that."

Again the environment shifted. They stood at the edge of the village, the woods a few hundred feet in front of them. "We'll follow the road."

Isabelle executed a series of micro-shifts, leap-frogging down a rough trail leading east through the woods. Emma felt no wind as they moved, but she felt the solid ground.

At last, they arrived at a hill overlooking a valley situated by the Hague River. Emma gasped.

A fortress loomed in front of them, tall wooden palisade ringing a stone keep. No guards manned the walls, but from what Isabelle had said, they wouldn't appear to their sight unless they got closer. "Did they build that?" she asked.

"I don't think so," Feodora said. "That is Landgren Keep, if I remember my history correctly. It existed from before the Founders and was where the natives of this land controlled the Hague River from."

"So not the Haguesfort?" Emma asked.

"No. The legends say Frederick Hague built the Haguesfort after the Founding."

"Keep holding hands," Isabelle warned. The landscape flickered again, and they stood in a courtyard beyond the walls, the keep in front of them. Here, a pair of guards also stood guard in front of the keep, while a patrol neared their location, both groups unable to see the girls. Another blink and they stood at the top of a set of stone steps. A pair of wooden doors barred their way.

"How do we get beyond? Can you shift blindly?"

"We can walk through," Isabelle said. "Feodora, keep holding my hand. Emma, let get of mine. I'll lead the line into the building."

Emma did as commanded and fell in behind Kylie, clutching her hand ever more tightly. She felt nothing out of the ordinary as they passed through the door - they might as well have been passing through mist.

They made their way through yet another set of closed doors and found themselves in an interior courtyard of the keep. Several levels of balconies overlooked their location.

"Where would they keep the prisoners?" Emma asked.

"Probably in the dungeon," Feodora said.

"Or in an upper room, so that it would be easier to protect them from rescue."

"They took teenagers, remember?" Emma pointed out. "They couldn't stash them all in private rooms. They'd have to hold them in the dungeons." It seemed logical to her.

"We'll try the basement first," Isabelle concluded, tugging them toward a set of stairs at the far end of the courtyard that seemed to slant downward instead of up like the stairs in the corners of the yard.

"Why is the ground solid but the doors not?" Emma asked as they traversed the short grass that remained immobile at their passing. "Or walls," she added.

"My mother says it has something to do with the permanence of an object. Things like walls and floors are permanent - fixed things. Doors are less permanent and can be opened at will or chopped down." Isabelle shrugged. "There's not an exact science to it, despite my father's attempts to explain it. We bend this world to our will, but we don't own it."

The girls made their way down two flights of stairs before emerging in a hallway. Here, two guards flanked the opening at the base of the steps. They took a right and then a left and found themselves in a guard room, for two guards sat at a table, making throwing motions with their hands that reminded Emma of playing cards. "Why can't we see the cards?" she asked.

Isabelle shrugged again. "Permanence of objects, I guess. You'll sometimes get flickers of the items, if you watch long enough, or out of the corner of your eye. It can be disconcerting if you dwell on it too long."

Emma took in a series of cells surrounding the guards. "Over there, I see some bodies." She pointed to their right.

Isabelle led them to the bars of a cage and then they passed through.

Emma knelt next to a girl curled up on the stone floor. She wore dirty clothes and did not appear to even have a blanket to cover herself. "The girls who were taken from the villages," Emma concluded.

"I think it's more than just the local girls," Kylie concluded. "There are two dozen cells here - and they're all as packed as this one."

"Let's find Ethan and Richard," Emma said.

"Shouldn't we do something about these girls?" Kylie protested. "We could rescue them."

"We can't take them all with us," Isabelle said. "Even if we *all* held hands, I don't have the power for that."

"We have to leave them behind," Feodora agreed. "But we can come back for them later, Kylie."

"But..."

"We're running out of time," Emma cut in. "Can you shift us out, Isabelle?"

"We should find Ethan and Richard first," Isabelle said. "Otherwise the guards will see us and could sound the alarm."

"Then we kill them," Feodora said. "You have your weapons. Emma and I have belt knives. Shift out behind them and we can stab them before they know what hit them."

"Come on," Isabelle said, leading the line. They walked the perimeter of the guard room, peering into each cage in the ever-present dull light of the shadow realm, but found only more of the same - girls, and some boys, in cages. No sign of Ethan or Richard.

"Maybe they're upstairs," Emma suggested. "Since they're higher profile."

"There's another door there," Kylie said, nodding toward an entry-way opposite the one they'd come in.

They walked through said door and found a hallway mirroring the one they'd come down, minus the stairs. Here no guards patrolled, but barred rooms lined the hall. They turned to the left and made their way along the line, searching each cell.

Finally, in the corner cell, a glint of metal caught Emma's eyes. "Wait. Follow me." She took the lead and stepped toward the shiny object that had caught her eye. A collar glimmered among a cluster of flesh. She bent down and Ethan's face, though battered, was there, eyes closed. Emma's breath caught. "It's him."

"And there's Richard," Kylie said, gesturing with her head to a larger boy laying closer to the corner.

"Shift us out, now," Emma commanded.

"Already on it," Isabelle said. Moments later the gray of the shadow realm gave way to the pitch darkness of a subterranean prison cell at night. Emma let go of Kylie's hand. *Ah, the comfort of the real world.*

"I'll make a light," Emma said, summoning heat to ignite the air and using her magic as fuel. A small flame sparked into existence above her spread hand. "Ethan," she whispered as loudly as she dared. "Ethan, Richard, wake up."

Ethan stirred, the dim light reflecting off his now-open eyes. "Emma? Am I dreaming?"

Emma sent the flame to the corner and pinned it there, then knelt beside her twin. "You're not dreaming. It's really me."

Richard stirred in the corner, sitting up but saying nothing.

Ethan groaned. "You shouldn't have come. You have to go, now."

Emma frowned. "But...we're here to rescue you."

"You don't understand," he said, coughing before continuing, his voice strained. "It's a trap."

A chill spread down Emma's spine. "What do you mean, a trap?"

"They used me as bait," he continued. "He knew you, Isabelle and Bridgette were there. He knew you would shift in."

"But that means...," Emma began.

A gong sounded from somewhere, reverberating through the stone walls and floor. At the same moment, Emma's flame extinguished. *What in the world is going on?* Emma thought. She reached for her magic but...it wasn't there.

"I can't use my magic," Kylie said.

"Neither can I," Feodora said.

"Quick, grab my hands," Isabelle urged.

Emma clutched at her brother, trying to find his hand. "Get up, Ethan. We have to go."

"It's too late," he said.

"They blocked your powers," Richard said from the corner.

"He's right," Isabelle said, hesitation in her voice. "I...I can't shift."

"No," Emma said in denial. "How are they suppressing our powers without collars?"

"That, my dear, is a secret," a deep male voice said from behind her.

Emma spun and found a man standing silhouetted against a dozen or more torches. "Who are you?"

"Oh, we've met," the man said. "Don't you recognize my voice?"

"Zerrecia," Kylie said, tremor in her voice.

"Yes," he said, slurring the s. "The same. Valdorf will be pleased when he hears we have captured some powerful souls. Take them."

Isabelle withdrew her dual daggers, while Emma and Feodora fumbled with their belt knives. Ethan and Richard, along with several of the other boys in the cage, stood up, though they seemed more wary. Had they tried to escape before?

Zerrecia laughed. "Your resistance is admirable - but futile." He waved forward.

Several guards advanced on the cell, silhouetted in the light of the torches held by their comrades.

The first guard through the door faced Isabelle, who charged toward him with dual blades. He tried to grab her arm, but she slashed upward and sliced into his arm, causing blood to splatter. However, two more guards restrained her arms. She kicked out at them but to no effect - without her powers and in such a confined space she was an ordinary teenage girl with some martial prowess facing daunting odds. Within moments, the guards had dragged her out of the cell.

Emma held her belt knife in a shaking hand. *Without my magic I have even less prowess than Isabelle.* Still, she hoped she could wound one of the guards.

Her hopes were dashed when she stabbed out at a guard and he brushed her arm aside. Then he punched her in the face. Pain blossomed in her skull and the darkness of unconsciousness took her.

Chapter 17

"Emma," a male voice came. "Emma, wake up."

Emma groaned but kept her eyes shut. "I don't want to get up, Dad."

"Is she delirious?" a girl asked.

"She got smacked in the head pretty good," another girl said.

"It's not Dad. It's Ethan."

"Ethan," she repeated, memory flooding back. Seventeen years with her twin, their departure from Ironforge, being captured by the Cult of Rae, training at the Tower, and now... "I remember." She remembered the girls too - Feodora, Isabelle and Kylie. She opened her eyes, squinting at the sunlight coming through a tiny window in the stone wall behind Ethan. She tried sitting up, but pain flared through her brain.

Shadow, she thought. *What's wrong with me?*

You have a concussion, Ma'am. I have redirected nanites to your brain to ensure no permanent damage ensues. The effects should wear off within a few minutes.

Thanks. Aloud, she groaned and closed her eyes. "My head."

"Just rest," Kylie said. Emma recognized her voice now. A hand pressed her shoulder back.

"Are Feodora and Isabelle okay?" she asked.

"I'm here," her friend said from a corner of the room. "A few bruises, but they didn't knock me out."

"You took the brunt of it," Ethan said. "Those bastards. But why did you girls come?"

"We had to rescue you," Emma protested, the throbbing in her head gradually subsiding.

"Great job we did of that," Isabelle said.

"My mother will get the note I left," Feodora said. "She'll send help."

"And fall into their trap too?" Isabelle countered.

Emma opened her eyes and gently moved Kylie's hand aside. "I can sit up." She suited action to words and looked around.

Isabelle indeed sat in the corner, while Kylie knelt next to Emma. Ethan knelt at her feet while Richard sat in a corner opposite Isabelle and Feodora paced the bedchamber they found themselves in. "Why aren't we down in the basement cells?" Emma asked.

"They said we were too 'high value' to leave down there," Feodora said with a sniff.

Emma reached for her magic but nothing came. She touched her neck, but no collar bound it. "How did they nullify our power?"

"I heard them talking about some kind of Krai'kesh artifact," Kylie said.

"Yeah, took ours off too," Ethan said, rubbing his neck. "Guess they trust whatever artifact is nullifying our power to keep doing it."

"Why..."

Her question was interrupted by the sound of the door unlocking and slamming open. A dozen or more guards swarmed in, wood clubs at the ready.

Emma tensed, considering resisting, but when she glanced at Isabelle her friend shook her head while maintaining eye contact, as if to say, "don't do it." Instead she thrust her wrists out for the guards to bind with rope. They then bound her to Kylie and Feodora with rope, making it even harder to escape.

Less than a minute after the guards had entered, they led the six mages out of their cell and down a winding staircase. The door at the bottom opened into the courtyard they'd seen the night before.

Sunlight illuminated dozens of girls and a few boys similarly bound together in a line. Whimpers and cries echoed from a few of the girls, while the rest stared on despondently. Emma and her companions did not join them, however, for the guards jerked them to a halt on the opposite side of the courtyard.

Guards armed with swords and shields ringed the courtyard, while more with loaded crossbows in hand watched from the balcony above.

They really don't want us escaping, Emma thought. Even if they were to break free of the grip of the guard holding the rope, they would be filled with crossbow bolts before they made it a few meters. Not to mention the fate that would await those who failed to escape.

The main door to the keep opened and Zerrecia entered, hood of his black cloak down. His eyes swept over the multitude of prisoners. Only when his eyes fell on Emma and her friends did he pause and smile. "Ah, good, everyone is here. Bring it in!" he shouted.

Four guards carried a wide stone ring into the courtyard. They placed the ring on the ground near the center of the yard, then stood it up and braced it with rocks on either side to keep it upright. Two guards remained at its side, holding the sides as well.

Zerrecia walked up to Emma specifically and lifted her chin with a finger. "So much power in such a small frame. Oh the trouble you and your friends have caused me and my master."

Isabelle spat. "I don't see your master here."

Emma eyed the stone ring to avoid thinking about the man's evil finger touching her skin, her stomach sinking. *That might be about to change.*

Indeed, Zerrecia removed his finger and gestured to the stone ring. It was as wide as the tallest man and had grooves or troughs gouged into the stone. "That will soon change."

"What do you have planned, you monster?" Emma demanded.

"Isn't it obvious?" the man asked. "A sacrifice must be made for my master to be returned to our world by our god, Rae'Shela. The blood of the innocent shall be shed this day to open the portal."

"How can you use magic when we cannot?" Feodora asked.

"Ah, thank you for the reminder, Princess," he replied haughtily. "The collars," he snapped his fingers and a pair of guards scrambled to place silver collars around their necks. "We wouldn't want you trying anything during the ceremony."

"You won't get away with this," Feodora said. "Even now my mother is on her way."

Just keep quiet, Emma thought. If he hadn't remembered the collars, they might have been able to fight back when they dropped the nullification field.

"Good, I look forward to seeing the look on her face when my master returns and destroys her puny army."

"The Eternals will stop you," Isabelle said.

"Oh? Of which you are one, are you not?" He chuckled. "You did a fantastic job of 'stopping' me last night, didn't you?"

Isabelle blushed.

"As for the rest, two of their number haven't been seen in twenty years."

"Since they defeated your master," Feodora boasted. "They're still out there, waiting."

"Yes, yes, I'm sure of it," he said mockingly. "More than likely, they died and the bureaucracy covered it up." He waved a hand. "No matter, though. This time, my master will have the tools to make him unstoppable."

What does he mean by that? Emma thought.

"But enough talk. Let the ritual begin! Disable the artifact!" He paused for a long moment as one of his minions departed to a room to one side of the keep. They returned moments later and Zerrecia withdrew a purple crystal the size of a short sword from his robes. Then, without preamble, he turned his back to Emma and her friends and held it toward the other teenagers.

"Vrom rae, vrom ro, sanguines withdrawos!" He pointed one end of the crystal toward the captured teens.

At first, nothing happened. Emma exchanged worried glances with Kylie. Would the magic affect them?

The crystal answered her silent question a moment later as it sparked to life, reddish-purple light flaring forth. Tendrils of energy matching the color of the crystal spread out like roots of a tree and began wrapping around the prisoners one-by-one.

Can they see the tendrils too? Emma wondered. Or was it like her own magic - invisible to the eyes of mundanes?

The first prisoner touched by the magic tendril fell to her knees, screaming and clutching at her head, then a second, then a third. Soon every prisoner had fallen to their knees and screamed. But the worst was yet to come.

The beam turned full red, and Emma realized this was no longer only visible to her - it was blood. Blood flowing out of the prisoners, along the tendrils of magic, and streaming into the crystal, which pulsed as though it were a human heart.

Emma's eyes widened and she put her hands over her mouth in horror. *They're killing them!* She looked to her left and found her friends sharing her expression. She took a step forward, but a guard shoved her back and she almost tumbled to the ground.

Bodies dropped one by one as the prisoners, drained of their blood, crumpled. The ritual seemed to go on forever, though Emma knew it was likely only a minute or two. She forced herself to watch as the last of the prisoners died. The streams of magic winked out of existence.

Zerrecia hoisted the now-red crystal and swung it in Emma's direction.

Emma closed her eyes, bracing for the inevitable. *He'll kill us too, to summon his master.* When she felt nothing, she peeked out.

The crystal had swung past her direction and pointed directly at the upright stone ring. "Vrom rae, vrom ro, sanguines offernos!"

This time, the red tendrils lashed out and attached to the circular frame of the stone ring. From Emma's vantage point, she saw the troughs on her side of the ring filling supernaturally with blood. *It should be falling to the ground, but it's not*, she thought. Perhaps his will held it in place against the pull of gravity.

The center of the ring glowed blood red, beginning as a pinprick and growing to encompass the entire space of the ring. The tendrils of magic winked out once more.

It's a portal, Emma realized as her breath caught. *They're summoning Valdorf through a portal.* Why hadn't they thought of that earlier?

For several long moments, nothing happened. But then, a foot emerged. The rest of his body followed and there stood Valdorf, black cloak billowing behind him and back to Emma and the others. Billows of what looked like the shadow energy Isabelle and Bridgette created when they shifted faded slowly around him. The red portal evaporated behind him.

He tilted his bald head up and breathed deep. "Ah, to smell fresh air again."

"You mean the smell of death," Ethan said.

Valdorf spun, red eyes seeking out the speaker. When his eyes alighted on Ethan, he smiled. "Ah, the prodigal son." They switched to Emma. "And the daughter."

"What do you want with us?" Emma asked.

Valdorf cocked his head to the side. "You don't know?"

Emma shook her head, forcing herself to maintain eye contact.

"You have a very...special...heritage. Your blood is the key to obtaining weapons I did not have access to the first time."

Special heritage? Emma thought. They were nobodies. Sure, they had magic, and they'd been granted nanites by the Staff of Agamar, not their heritage.

"What weapons?" Feodora asked.

"All shall be revealed in time, Princess," he said with a smirk.

"Why are they here, then?" Emma asked, pointing to Kylie, Feodora and Isabelle. "If you only need Ethan and I, why don't you let them go?"

"Oh, they still hold value to me, child. One," he pointed to Isabelle, "is the daughter of the one who imprisoned me. One," he pointed to Feodora, "is the daughter of the queen of Tar Ebon. And the last," he pointed to Kylie, "is motivation for you. Fail to do as I say, when I say it, and your friend dies."

Kylie gasped, whether out of fear of dying or horror at the thought of being used as motivation, Emma didn't know.

"Now, let us begin. We have a journey to undertake." He did not leave the courtyard, however, but instead turned to Zerrecia. "The crystal." He held out his hand.

His lieutenant handed him the crystal, which still pulsed with light, if slightly dimmer.

"Bring forth the power source!" Valdorf commanded, his voice booming.

Four guards carried a metal cylinder out from a doorway and placed it on the ground in front of Valdorf.

What is that thing? Emma thought.

It is a shadow generator, Shadow replied. *Used to channel...*

I remember now. It's what they stole from Seaholme.

"With these tools, we can travel anywhere," Valdorf said. "Anywhere I have been, anyway, which would normally present a problem. Fortunately, the path to our destination has a secret access point. You're going home, twins."

Emma's eyes widened. Going back to Ironforge? Why? *What secret access point?* What was he after? "Why are you telling us all this?" she asked.

"Because there is nothing you can do to stop me, of course. I want you to understand, here," he touched his chest, "that you are powerless."

"Then why don't you tell us where you're taking us?"

"Oh. Zerrecia didn't tell you? We are going to the Halls of Light, of course!"

Emma's stomach sank. Of course. A technological fortress atop a mountain would be the perfect prize for him.

"What will you do to Ironforge?" she asked.

"If they open their gates and let my army pass, nothing. But if they resist," he grinned evilly, "then I will burn the city to the ground. Not even your parents will be able to stop me."

Our parents are nobodies, Emma thought. *Why would he keep mentioning them?*

"Wait," Isabelle said, stepping forward. "I've been to the Halls of Light and I too can manipulate shadow energy. Allow me to open the portal."

Valdorf quirked an eyebrow up. "How do I know you will not deceive me? Open the portal into the midst of the sea or some such place?"

"I'll go through first," Emma said. "She wouldn't risk my life."

"You're right, she wouldn't." He stroked his chin. "Fine. But if you try anything," he pointed at Emma, "her throat gets cut." He snapped his fingers and one of the guards drew his belt knife and placed it against Emma's throat. "She will be the first through, and if it is not the Halls, she dies."

Isabelle straightened. "I give you my word."

"Very well. Approach," he gestured to the cylinder in front of him. "Touch the generator, while holding this crystal, point it at the portal and envision a location within the Halls of Light. Then say these words: 'Vrae opendicus sae shadowcus.'"

Isabelle approached and grabbed the crystal. "I understand."

"Good. Then begi...," he trailed off as alarm bells tolled in the distance. "It seems your allies may have come to attempt a rescue."

"I shall lead the defense," Zerrecia said, bowing.

"No, you fool. Gather your elite troops and bring them here. Let the fodder hold them off while we go for the true prize."

"Yes, Master." If he felt any remorse at letting possibly hundreds of cultists die, he did not show it.

"Begin," Valdorf commanded, pointing at Isabelle.

"The collar," Isabelle said, touching the silver necklace. "It must be removed before I can use my power."

"So be it. But if you try anything," he again pointed to Emma, "she dies. Remember that. So much as fade to mist or draw upon your magic and her blood will soak the ground."

"I understand," Isabelle said again, this time through what sounded like clenched teeth.

Valdorf ran a hand over the collar and it clicked open. "Begin," he commanded again.

Isabelle closed her eyes and raised the crystal with one hand while touching the shadow generator with the other. "Vrae opendicus sae shadowcus," she intoned. The glow of the crystal intensified, while the shadow generator came to light, casting an eerie purple glow across the courtyard and causing Emma to shield her eyes for a moment.

A purple glow crept up Isabelle's arm and soon encompassed her entire body. It flowed down the arm holding the crystal and seemed to mingle with the reddish glow of the crystal to form a third color. Then a beam of light, rather than tendrils, shot forth from the tip of the crystal and stopped at the center of the portal, as if it had hit a wall. It was then the light split, splaying out like webs of a spider and connecting to the frame of the portal. The webs of light spread until the entire area of the ring glowed with the eerie reddish-purple light. The beam of light winked out and Isabelle fell to the ground.

"Isabelle!" Emma shouted, wishing she could run to her friend but restrained by the threat of having her throat cut.

"Take her through the portal," Valdorf commanded, gesturing to Emma with a back-handed wave.

"Move," the guard growled, marching her forward. Fortunately, Emma confirmed Isabelle continued to breath. The guard stopped her and turned her to face the portal, back to Valdorf and Isabelle. Then he shoved her ahead of him as the portal loomed.

Emma stepped through the portal.

Chapter 18

The center of the Halls of Light looked identical to the last time Emma had set foot in the place. The same orb floated high above, several other orbs orbiting it like planets around a sun.

The guard kept the knife in front of her throat while he looked around. "These them?" he asked.

"Yes," Emma said.

He stuck his head back through the portal, and Emma considered attempting escape. She envisioned slipping out from beneath the knife, kicking him and running for her life. But then the image of her friends being killed for her disobedience muscled its way into her mind and she stopped.

His head returned a few moments later. "The rest are on their way."

Following his words, Valdorf and Zerrecia entered. Then came Emma's brother and three friends, Isabelle limping with a hand to her head, each with a guard watching their every move. Finally, dozens of mages and at least a couple hundred soldiers streamed through.

Likely the remainder of their garrison, Emma thought.

When the last soldier had come through, the light from the portal winked out of existence, leaving only a stone arch in its place.

A beam of light shot out from a nearby wall and formed into the imagine of Al, the artificial intelligence that oversaw the Halls of Light. "Welcome to the Halls of Light," he said, smile on his face. "Welcome back, Mistress Emma, Mistress Isabelle."

Emma opened her mouth, intending to shout a warning, but the guard, perhaps expecting that move, inched the blade closer and drew blood.

"Quiet," he warned.

Emma snapped her mouth shut. *There must be a way to communicate with him. Wait. Shadow? Can you communicate with Al? Like Dawyn did with us?*

I can certainly attempt to establish a communication link, he replied. *One moment.* A heartbeat passed. *I have connected.*

Al, this is Mistress Emma. Can you hear me?

"Show us to the command center," Valdorf ordered aloud.

Al ignored him, replying instead to Emma via her implant. *I am receiving your signal, Mistress Emma. How may I help you?*

We are being held prisoner, she said. *Can you enable defenses? The man who spoke is named Valdorf, and he wants access to weapons of the Halls of Light. We can't let him.*

I shall activate intrusion alarms and send out a distress call to those equipped with reception technology.

Emma sagged in relief. *Thank you. We have to hold him off until reinforcements arrive.*

"I am afraid I cannot comply," Al said aloud. "I have been informed you have hostile intent. My own analysis of the state Mistress Emma and Mistress Isabelle find themselves in corroborates this allegation. I am activating defense mechanisms." His image winked out of existence.

BRIDGETTE SLID HER knife from the eye socket of a cultist and fluidly spun and stabbed another who was fighting one of the queen's knights in the back of the neck. That soldier dropped his weapon and shield and clutched at his throat as he crumpled to the ground. She took a moment to survey the scene.

The gates had been torn open by Jason, allowing the queen's knights to charge in, while the reinforcements she'd brought from Tar Ebon had scaled the walls and hurled their own barrage of arrows and bolts toward their foes atop the walls.

I must find Isabelle and the others, she thought grimly. Yet there was a barrier of darkness surrounding the keep. Within the shadow realm she could *see* the space beyond said darkness, but she could not pass that rift. It was as if it were a solid wall stretching skyward. *How did they manipulate energy nullification technology in such a precise manner?* Her understanding of the tech was that it was a blanket approach - either everything in an area was nullified or nothing was. But this...a barrier around an area where magic *was* possible - that was a new experience for her.

ALERT, ALERT, a voice boomed in her mind. *THE HALLS OF LIGHT HAVE BEEN BREACHED BY HOSTILE FORCES. I RE-PEAT - THE HALLS OF LIGHT HAVE BEEN BREACHED. ALL AVAILABLE FORCES PLEASE RESPOND.*

Shit, Bridgette thought. *I have to find Dawyn.* She shifted into the shadow realm and materialized down near the center of the courtyard, in front of the keep and right before the black barrier. She found him there, facing off against three cultists. He blurred and cut them down in a moment, then turned and saw Bridgette. "Did you hear it too?" he called.

Bridgette nodded in answer. It had been so loud she could barely hear. "I am going to get them," she called back, not wasting energy walking to him. "We'll need them if Valdorf has escaped." Indeed, the minute she'd seen the note Feodora left for the queen, Bridgette had dreaded what the cultists might want with a shadow generator and all those young people they'd snatched from their homes. It hadn't happened in just one area either - from as far south as Henry's Crossing they'd been taken and marched in secret north. Dawyn's rangers and the army had intercepted several groups of them, but they'd spread out to avoid suspicion and the countryside was vast. *Blood magic is one of the only ways he'd be able to escape the shadow realm,* she thought.

Her brother nodded. "Go!" he shouted.

Bridgette shifted to the shadow realm.

HIDDEN COMPARTMENTS along the walls slid aside and metal constructs in the shape of men stepped out. At least a dozen of the metal golems moved toward Valdorf's forces.

What are those things? Emma thought.

They are automatons, also known as 'robots,' Al said in her mind. She'd forgotten he was still connected.

I wish I had my magic right about now, Emma thought. Isabelle had hers, but that would do them little good. Still, she used the distraction to slam her head back into her guard's chest. She cringed in pain, but it accomplished what she'd hoped - the guard stumbled back and lowered the knife. She leapt to the side to avoid the blade and spun around, then kicked the man in the groin.

Her friends, taking notice of her action, followed suit in their own ways. Isabelle shifted to mist, Feodora stepped on her keeper's foot, Kylie elbowed her guard, Ethan turned and punched his in the face, while Richard grabbed his guard's arm and flipped him over his shoulder.

Isabelle reappeared behind a guard, grabbed his belt knife and slit his throat. Then she disappeared again.

I believe I can assist with that, Al replied. *Please hold still.*

Emma froze.

A beam of light, similar to that which had animated Al, shot out from a projector built into the wall. She looked down and it appeared to have connected with her collar. The collar made a clicking sound and fell to the ground.

Other beams of light shot out toward the others and in rapid succession the other four had their collars off.

Sweet magic flowed through Emma's mind.

Valdorf and his forces had not been idle. His guards formed ranks to face the robots, while the numerous mages he had brought along were hurling spells toward the constructs. Valdorf himself sent a stream of fire toward one, turning it into slag. "Their collars are off!" he shouted when his gaze fell upon Emma. He pointed and several of his mages, including Zerrecia, turned to face Emma and her allies. He remained focused on the oncoming machines.

The first mage hurled a ball of flame at Emma, which she deflected. He then shifted tactic and sent lightning streaming her way, but she redirected it into the stone at her feet.

I have to counter-attack, she thought, hurriedly thinking of spells. She launched a fireball toward him to give her time to think, which he dissolved in mid-flight. She followed it with a single shard of ice which she splintered mid-flight, sending a hail of smaller shards toward her foe. He summoned a wall of flame and in response she sent a stream of lightning dancing across the shards. The shards hit the wall of flame and melted, sending electrified water splattering onto the enemy mage and knocking him out.

Her friends were likewise holding their own, with Isabelle dancing from foe-to-foe, Kylie and Feodora linking together to use their magic and Ethan and Richard doing likewise. Still, Valdorf had dozens of mages and hundreds of soldiers at his disposal.

A flash of movement caught her eye. Across the massive central atrium figures, not mechanical figures, but people, appeared as if out of thin air. Except tendrils of shadow energy floated up around them.

Emma strained to see who they were, then almost took a sword in the gut as a guard took advantage of her distraction. She dispatched him with a fireball to the face, then returned to stare at the commotion.

"Valdorf!" a male voice shouted. "Give up, you can't win!"

Why does that voice sound so familiar? Emma thought. This time, neither Al nor Shadow answered her.

Valdorf, who had just dispatched two robots with a flaming sword, paused. Then he burst into laughter. "Oh John, my old nemesis. It *has* been too long."

"Not long enough," the man, John, replied. "In fact, seeing you here is too soon."

"The Halls hold what was stolen from me. You shall not keep me from it."

"Oh, so *this* is where Bridgette hid the gauntlet," John shouted back. "Well, you're not getting it, you big buffoon."

"Enough of this," Valdorf snapped. "Vrom rae, vrom roe, Rae'Shela accessio," he intoned, lifting his hands skyward.

What is he summoning now? Emma thought.

The sky turned black in an instant, as if something had blocked out the sun. Then, red lightning shot down from the blackened sky and toward his hand. There it swirled down his arm and then coalesced into...something.

A staff? Emma thought as it took on a more defined form, with a lightning bolt shape at the bottom, a twisting red pattern like a ribbon swirling along the haft. Four brown tendrils, each a couple of feet long, wriggled from the tip of the staff.

Gross, Emma thought.

"I no longer require the gauntlet. My god rewards my service with his unlimited power!"

"There's only one god," a female voice shouted back from across the hall. "And yours is *not* him!"

Emma blinked. She knew that voice. Knew it like she knew her own. "Mom?" she whispered.

"You shall know the truth soon enough. My god prepares to breach the firmament and consume your galaxy. His ships of living stone shall sail across the void and destroy the creations of Yahweh."

"Over our dead bodies," the man shouted, and Emma recognized it now.

"Dad," she whispered, tears in her eyes. What were her parents doing there? She sought out Ethan, who stood equally dumbfounded. He met her eyes and mouthed "dad." She nodded.

"In fact," her father continued. "Let's give you a little light show." In that moment, an astonishing surge of magic erupted from her father, manifesting as a flare of light. Light flowed from within the orbs floating above their heads as though it were a river and her father were at the base of the funnel. The brightness of the flare amplified. Then he leveled his arms toward Valdorf, hands forming a cup.

If Valdorf were worried, he showed no sign. Instead, he pointed the tip of the staff toward her father.

A beam of light shot from between her father's hands and barreled straight toward his foe. However, the brown tendrils that had until that point been waving in a seemingly random pattern spread wide to form an X and, in the center, an inky black circle formed to absorb the beam of light. A moment later it dissolved.

Shit, Emma thought.

"As you can see, my time in exile has not been for naught," Valdorf continued. "And now, to bring forth some of my friends." This time, he pointed the staff angled toward the floor and a portal formed a dozen feet from the tip. At first, nothing happened. Then, a claw emerged, and another, and then an upright torso, two arms with claws at either end and a pair of pincers surrounding a mouth full of sharp teeth. Two rear legs came last and there stood a creature of nightmare.

"A krai'kesh," Emma whispered to herself. A creature that hadn't been seen in twenty years stood before them, and it wasn't alone. Two more followed it through the portal, then two more and two more and soon Emma lost count as a torrent of the clawed creatures erupted from the darkness. They were not idle, either, for several charged toward the group her father stood with, others went toward the robots, but some also turned toward the cultists behind Valdorf.

"Master, the beasts are attacking us," Zerrecia called as one of the krai'kesh leapt toward one of his men.

"I told you your men were fodder, Zerrecia," Valdorf pronounced. "You too have served your purpose and shall reap your reward in the afterlife."

Zerrecia stood as still as a stone pillar, most likely in shock. "But...," he began.

"Emma, look out!" Ethan shouted.

She turned in time to see one of the monsters skittering toward her. Her eyes widened and she hastily summoned a barrier of air and superheated the air to ignite it. She watched with relief as the beast caught on fire after slamming into it.

Two krai'kesh charged Zerrecia. He screamed as the first stabbed him in the chest and the other sliced off his legs.

Ethan, Feodora, Kylie and Richard had formed a semi-circle and threw offensive spells toward any krai'kesh that came near, though they were insulated by the foot soldiers and mages under Zerrecia's command. Said minions fought for their lives in light of the betrayal by their master.

That doesn't make us allies, Emma thought. There was a saying her father used to use, "the enemy of my enemy is my friend," but she was sure it didn't apply here. *They'll as soon gut us as they will the krai'kesh.*

Isabelle appeared beside Emma. "Take my hand," she said.

Emma grasped it without thinking and a moment later found herself in the gray of the shadow realm. The battle continued to rage on, only in greyscale. "Where are we going?" she asked.

"To find the Gauntlet of Eramicea," her friend announced.

"But...where are we going to find it?"

"I asked my mother. She told me where it is." The scene flashed and they found themselves at the gate leading to one of the wings surrounding the center hall like spokes of a wheel. "I can't pass through the gate. We have to shift out." Emma felt a tugging feeling and color returned, along with the distant sound of steel and screams and the smell of char and blood.

"How do we get in?" Emma asked, studying the gilded door. "This is the restricted section."

"I can help," Al said from behind them. He stood with his hands clasped in front of him as if there were not a battle for the fortress he managed raging in the central hall. "The door requires a blood sacrifice."

"More blood magic," Emma grumbled. Hadn't there been enough blood magic for one day? It wasn't even noon and Valdorf had emerged from the shadow realm thanks to blood magic, then used it to open a portal to the Halls of Light. "Fine. Do we just put our hands on the door or what?"

"Yes," he said. A panel on the door slid open to reveal a circular hole about the size of a fist. "Place your hand inside, palm down."

Emma eyed the hole but didn't question any further. She held her hand out as instructed and thrust it in. Cool metal met her skin. At first nothing happened, and Emma let out her breath. But then, "ow," she exclaimed as something poked the soft flesh of her middle finger. A glass ring around the hole glowed white for a moment and spun around the circumference of the opening before changing to green color. The door made a clicking sound.

"Access granted," Al said. "You may withdraw your hand."

Emma did, and found the pin-prick caused by gaining access to the door already being healed. *Thank you, Shadow.*

The doors swung inward as though doormen had opened them from the inside. Together she and Isabelle passed over the threshold. The doors then closed of their own accord moments later.

Locked in, Emma thought. *It's alright, my blood will get us out again.*

They found themselves in a cavernous room with golden pedestals of varying heights scattered throughout. Atop each pedestal sat a glass box. The glass boxes held a wide variety of artifacts, ranging from small metal boxes to orbs with what looked like storm clouds floating within them to what looked like a golden pitchfork with the central spike being longer than the other two. And there, in the center of the room, sat a black glove with a dark mist even now surrounding it.

Emma gasped. "That has to be it," she said, pointing to draw her friend's attention to it.

Together they approached the pedestal holding the glove. Emma touched the glass and this time, instead of a prick, she felt a jolt of lightning, or electricity, as Shadow would name it, flow up her arm briefly. Then the glass case retracted its top and descended into the pedestal.

"You use it," Isabelle insisted.

"But...it looks like shadow magic," Emma protested. "That's your specialty. You're the shadow mage."

"And you're the stronger regular mage," Isabelle pointed out. "Sure, I can use some magic, but I'm no match to your strength."

"Do we know what the gauntlet does?" Emma asked.

"My mother said it grants some power like mine. I don't know how strong. We don't have time to argue. Put on the gauntlet."

Emma eyed the gauntlet. Her friend...her cousin...was right. "All right." She grabbed the black glove and, taking a deep breath, inserted her right hand into it.

A surge of energy shot down her arm, much like it had when she'd touched the glass containing the gauntlet, but this time it was accompanied by a burning sensation and a black mist that encompassed her arm and then the rest of her body.

Terragenesis detected, Shadow warned. *Shall I deploy countermeasures?*

No, Emma said. *I need its power.*

I must warn you, Ma'am, that prolonged use of this device is likely to cause irreparable damage to your body.

I don't care, Emma replied. The effect subsided visually, though Emma could still feel the power thrumming under her skin. She smiled at Isabelle, who frowned. "It worked. I'm fine."

"Okay, let's get back. Take my hand." Her cousin extended her hand.

"Let me try to shift on my own," Emma replied. She closed her eyes. *Shift!* Nothing happened. She opened her eyes. "Ummm...how do I shift?"

"We can't shift in here," Isabelle explained. "There's a nullification field in place. We have to go beyond those doors," she pointed to the doors through which they'd entered, "and then we can."

Together they ran back to the doors they'd entered earlier. This time they required no blood sacrifice and opened at their approach. *Apparently, they don't care who leaves the archives*, Emma thought.

"Okay, now how do I shift?" she asked as they stood in the hall.

"It's like you have to feel the power inside you and then envision it encompassing you and it's like your body drifts into the shadow realm. That's the best way I can explain it."

Emma closed her eyes again, exhaling as she did. *Just stay calm.* She focused on the new thrumming, pulsing power and "harnessed" it with her mind. Then she did as Isabelle had instructed and envisioned her body fading to mist, as though she were steam or an early morning fog. The effect was immediate - she recognized the feel of shifting from Isabelle doing it. She opened her eyes again and found herself in the greyscale representation of the hall of artifacts.

Isabelle still stood in front of her, there in the flesh too, smiling. "You did it!" she exclaimed.

"I feel invincible," Emma said. "Let's go kick Valdorf's ass."

"Here, I'll help guide us back," Isabelle said, offering her hand once again. Emma took it and in the blink of an eye they were back in the main hall where the battle raged on. "Where do we want to come out at?" she asked.

Emma considered either by Ethan and her friends or over by her parents. "By Ethan." They would likely need the most help, what with being surrounded by cultists *and* facing the krai'kesh warriors.

The scene flashed and they were standing behind Feodora. "Where's Kylie?" Emma asked. Her friend wasn't there in the circle.

"I'll bring us out," Isabelle said, then color returned to the world before Emma could protest that she wanted to try herself.

Having sensed a presence, Feodora spun around. "Emma! Isabelle! Where did you go?" Her voice held a mix of relief and terror.

"We had to get this," Emma said, holding up her right hand which held the gauntlet. "It's going to even the odds."

"Good, because we could use some evening right about now," Ethan said over his shoulder. "Those things just keep coming. Mom and Dad and the others are holding their own for now, but nothing they throw at Valdorf even touches him. And now without Kylie..."

"Without Kylie," Emma repeated. "Where is she?"

Ethan pointed. "He has her."

Emma turned her gaze to Valdorf for the first time since re-entering the room. Then she gasped. Kylie floated in front of him, tendrils from the staff wrapped around her entire body to the point that only her head remained visible. Those same tendrils held her several feet aloft. Her eyes were closed, but her face was pale.

"No!" Emma screamed, her anguished cry somehow cutting through the din of combat. Her best friend, even closer to her than Feodora or Isabelle, who she now knew was family, was in the clutches of the enemy. Was she even alive?

Valdorf, hearing her scream, turned, red eyes alighting upon her. "Ah," he shouted, "the prodigal daughter returns!"

"And this time I don't come empty-handed," she said, voice still amplified. She lifted her arm and formed the gauntlet into a fist. *Is the gauntlet amplifying my voice?*

Valdorf chuckled. "A child's toy compared to the power *I* wield. Now," he swept his arm out to indicate her and her friends, "kneel and my god may allow you to repent."

"Never," Emma said, clenching her teeth.

Her foe shrugged. "Very well." He swung his staff and Kylie swung with it, tentacles still wrapped around her body. "Then I shall offer your friend." He thrust Kylie into the dark portal, held her there for a heart-beat and when he removed the staff, she was gone.

Emma had no words in that moment. She roared in wordless fury and drew upon all her magic plus the magic of the gauntlet she now felt in the back of her mind. *My best friend, and I didn't even get to say good-bye. What anguish will she endure at the hands of Rae'Shela?* She formed a spell in her mind; flame, but dark, twisted. She lifted her hands and the beam of searing black heat slashed toward Valdorf.

He again lifted the staff and a small portal opened to absorb the en-ergy. "Is that all you have, child? Give up - you cannot defeat me."

"Maybe not alone," Ethan said, stepping up beside Emma. "But she's not alone." He turned his head to her and offered his hand. "Take my hand, and my magic."

Emma smiled, the love for her brother easing the pain of loss slight-ly. She clasped his hand.

"And mine," Feodora said, stepping up on Emma's left.

"Me too," Richard said, taking Ethan's other hand.

"Ah, Hell, if we're going to die might as well die fighting," Isabelle said, grabbing Feodora's hand.

Tears trickled down Emma's cheeks, though she continued to glare at Valdorf.

A gust of air caused her to turn her head to look over her shoulder. Her parents, along with her Uncle Jason, Aunt Bridgette and Dawyn, stood there along with the remaining soldiers they'd brought.

"You're never alone, Emma," her mother said, smiling.

"Well, until we die, one day," her father said, shrugging.

Her mother punched him in the shoulder.

"Ow. Okay, when we die, which will be a long, long time from now. Hopefully," he added in a quieter tone.

Emma smiled in spite of herself. The knowledge of her father's true identity hadn't dampened her appreciation of his humor. "Thank you. Now lend me your magic, all of you."

First Ethan, then Feodora, then the others in her circle stretched out with their magic to send it flowing into Emma. Then her parents and her uncle sent their power, and Emma started. Immense flows, as wide as rivers compared to her creek, swirled around her, waiting to be drawn upon.

You can do this, Emma thought to herself, trying to bolster her confidence. *They're all behind you.*

This time, Emma drew more upon the shadow energy granted by the gauntlet. She formed it into a floating ball two feet in front of her chest. Then she drew upon the elemental magic granted by her family and friends and filled the orb with the magic. Everything she had poured into it. *If this fails, we will have no energy left.*

When the orb was full, with glimmers of fire and white light breaking through the outer shell of darkness, Emma cast it forward as though it were a ball she was throwing to a friend. It moved slow at first, but then picked up speed.

Valdorf again summoned the portal of darkness like before.

This time, Emma split the master orb into four. The four orbs circumvented the portal and then she merged them again and watched with satisfaction as it collided with Valdorf's chest. The darkness swept around her foe, like a cloud, and the energy within exploded outward, enveloping him at once in fire and ice and air and light. He screamed and flew backward to land on his back in front of the portal he'd summoned.

His staff fell from his hand and rolled. "Im...possible..." he gasped. "My god..."

Emma breathed a sigh of relief. *It's finished.* Still, she drew again on what little strength remained and prepared a final spell if he got up.

Movement in the portal caught her eye. Tendrils resembling those on his staff, only formed of dark mist, streaked out and wrapped around his body. Then, before Emma could even react, the tendrils had lifted Valdorf up and pulled him through.

"What the hell," Ethan said.

"That can't be good," Emma's father said.

Did he die, or did his god save him? Emma wondered silently.

The portal widened and this time the tendrils returned but formed the shape of...something.

"What is that?" Emma asked aloud.

"Like I said, nothing good," her father said.

"Destroy it before it has time to fully form," Bridgette ordered.

"Okay," Emma said. *But what is it?* She unleashed the power she'd been mustering upon it in the form of shadow-infused lightning. It sliced through the coalescing form but the moment the lightning ceased the shadowy shape returned to its original shape.

As if feeding on her defeat, the shadowy figure took on flesh. It was human, but...not. He looked like a male, from the neck up, then his torso and arms looked human, while from the waist down he looked like one of the krai'kesh monstrosities. On top of that, four other appendages curved out from his back and ending in three-pointed claws which clacked together as he gazed on them with eyes of pure black.

"At last, I have breached the firmament," he said, booming voice sounding like a mix of human and insect. Dark mist swirled around it like breath in the cold.

"That is the ugliest thing I've ever seen," Emma's father said.

"What is it?" Ethan asked.

"I am the avatar of Rae'Shela," the being boomed. "I am the doom of your world."

"How are we going to defeat *that*?" Feodora asked.

"We..." Emma stopped as an orange light from above caught her attention.

Two orange portals formed in the dark sky above them. At first, only the eerie orange glow was visible, but then trumpets sounded as if from all around, causing Emma to cover her ears.

At last, she could see two figures descending as though being lowered by rope to the ground. They too possessed human faces, though the details were obscured by an orange-white aura. But in addition to hands and feet, six wings sprouted from their backs, fluttering in the air.

They touched down between Emma'a group and this new being. "Breach detected," they said in unison. "Initiating defense mechanism."

"No..." the avatar protested, stepping back. "You should not be here."

The newcomers did not reply. Instead, as one, they lifted their arms, fingers splayed, and four beams of pure white light shot forth and connected with the chest of the avatar.

The creature screamed as the light penetrated it and began to glow from beneath its skin. Then, its body exploded physically, light flaring out, and body parts flew in every direction.

A claw skidded to a halt at Emma's feet, green blood seeping from it. She covered her mouth in a vain attempt to not vomit.

Their duty done, the beings of light turned to Emma and her group. "Prepare, mortals," they began, voices booming in unison, "for the invasion of the dark beings."

"When will they come?" Dawyn asked.

"The hour is not yet set," they responded. "But their journey will soon begin. Prepare for their coming."

"And will you come to fight alongside us when they come?" Dawyn pressed.

"Should you call upon us, we may come once more," they each raised an arm and pointed a finger at Emma. Or the gauntlet, she wasn't sure. "Prepare." Then, they rose again, six wings each flapping in the air, and ascended to the orange portals hovering in the sky. Moments later, the portals winked out of existence and the clouds parted to allow the early morning sun to stream in.

Chapter 19

Reality gradually returned to normal in the aftermath of the beings of light flying skyward and the portals or whatever they were closing. *What* was *that portal? And what were those things?* Emma thought. She looked to her father and raised an eyebrow.

"Hey, don't look at me, kid," he said, shrugging. "Your uncle's the man of science. I'm just the handsome one."

Despite everything that had happened, the losses and destruction, Emma had to chuckle at her father's good humor.

The remaining soldiers set about dragging the krai'kesh and cultist corpses into piles while shackling the surviving cultists. The fallen soldiers were laid out in a neat row.

"Well, Jason," Emma's mother said, an hour later. Emma's family and friends stood near one of the windows overlooking the planet below. "Any idea what the hell just happened today?"

"It looked like a dimensional portal," Emma's Uncle Jason began. "Like it sucked Valdorf through. And then...well..." he stopped, seemingly at a loss for words.

"An avatar of a 'god' came through," Emma's aunt Bridgette said.

"Then angels came down," John chimed in. "Or at least, they sure as heck looked like it." He looked skyward. "Maybe the big guy was looking out for us."

"Then extra-dimensional beings appeared and closed the portal," Uncle Jason concluded. "Or perhaps it was a breach and they acted like..." he waved his hands vaguely, "...a defense mechanism of some sort."

"Like anti-bodies against an infection," Emma's mother said.

"They were seraphim," Aunt Bridgette put in.

"We don't know that for certain," Uncle Jason put in.

"Sera-what?" Emma's father put in.

"Seraphim," Bridgette repeated. "Fiery angels mentioned in the Bible during the visions sent to Isaiah. The description in the Bible matches what we saw." She lifted a finger. "First, the flame." A second finger rose. "Second, the six wings."

"Kind of flimsy evidence," Emma's mother replied.

"I met someone...once before," Aunt Bridgette said. "Nearly twenty years ago in Shar'hai. He...he claimed to be God. Or Jesus. And the way he was only visible to me and disappeared...unless he was a shifter there was no way he could do that. And he could see me in the shadow realm."

"Could you have been partaking in some desert weed?" Emma's father asked, miming smoking a pipe.

"I wasn't hallucinating," Aunt Bridgette snapped, "if that's what you're implying."

Her father held his hands up. "Hey, no judgment."

Aunt Bridgette gritted her teeth but did not reply.

"I doubt all of us mass hallucinated," Emma's father said, in defense of his wife. "The exact identity of the beings may remain a mystery, however."

"So is Valdorf not dead?" Emma asked, shuddering.

"He's dead, honey," her mother said, walking over to her and embracing her. "Your attack worked. His god only withdrew a corpse, I'm sure of it. He's gone for good this time."

Emma nodded, feeling somewhat relieved. *What if he's not? I must try not to dwell on it.*

"So what's next?" Ethan said. "Like, with this place?"

"That's what we're here to decide," Dawyn said. He'd been looking out the glass viewport at the world below, his back to the group, but now turned to face them. "The weapons in this place - the power of it - the world is not ready for these things. We came this close," he pinched his thumb and pointer finger together to the point where only a tiny amount of space remained, "to a world-ending event. If we'd failed, the Krai'kesh would be guaranteed victory when they return."

No one spoke for a long moment as the gravity of the situation settled on each of them, like a heavy blanket being thrown over the room.

"If the Halls were to fall into the hands of the Empire," he continued, "and we were unable to pull off a defense like today fast enough, they could finish what Valdorf started."

"Would they really risk destroying themselves too?" Emma's mother said.

"Many weapons here could be used to only target Tar Ebon or a single continent. Correct, Jason?"

Uncle Jason shrugged. "There would be environmental impacts, but yes, a single nuke could wipe out Tar Ebon without affecting the imperial continent."

"Then they could sail in and impose their will on the remnants of the Federation," Dawyn pointed out. "That is a risk we cannot take."

"So what, we just destroy the weapons?" Emma's mother asked.

"Or use them on the Empire," Aunt Bridgette said.

Emma's father pointed to the woman. "She's got a point. End them before they can end us."

Her mother, who had disengaged from Emma and rejoined her husband, punched him in the shoulder. "We're not in the business of genocide!" She looked to Dawyn. "What do you suggest?"

"There's another option," Uncle Jason interrupted as the supreme commander opened his mouth to speak.

"We're listening," Dawyn said.

"The Halls have an extra-planetary feature. Remember, this was once an orbital station which was landed on the top of this mountain. It's *designed* to orbit a planet and deploy its communication arrays."

"So why didn't the Founders do that?" Emma blurted out, then blushed. What business did she, a mage who hadn't even started her second year of training at the Tower, have questioning her brilliant uncle?

"That's a good question," Uncle Jason said, pointing at her and smiling.

"Do you know the answer?" Ethan asked, emboldened by his sister.

"Judging by the creation of the shadow gate mechanism to reach this place, they intended to use it in dire circumstances."

"Such as when the Krai'kesh emerged?" Dawyn asked. "No record of it existed when they showed their ugly faces."

Uncle Jason shrugged. "It was a thousand-year gap, Dawyn. Perhaps the knowledge was intercepted."

"Or purposely suppressed," Aunt Bridgette said. "The Cult of Rae seems to trace its origins back to the Founding. Perhaps they couldn't reach the Halls, so they buried the knowledge."

"Based upon what we know of their motivations," Dawyn said, "that's a good theory." He cleared his throat. "I for one vote to send this into orbit as intended. It keeps the weapons out of reach of zealots while not destroying them. You heard those seraphim; we have to prepare for an invasion."

"Out of reach for how long?" Aunt Bridgette argued. "How long before we have a space program?"

Emma furrowed her brow. She'd seen a lot of things in the past year, but space? "A space program?"

"We're several centuries from launching anything man-made into orbit," Uncle Jason said, ignoring Emma's question, "let alone a moon landing. That's *with* the knowledge in my head. The Halls are an exceptional case in that they were manufactured using methods that are beyond even where we came from."

"Wait," Ethan put in, catching up to Emma. "So people can actually go into space?"

"Yeah, kid," their father began. "Where we come from, men and women called astronauts flew in space shuttles into space. They flew to the moon, up to space stations, and were even planning a manned mission to Mars."

"Not to mention the many probes and deep-space satellites sent out into the void to take pictures of distant solar systems and galaxies," Uncle Jason said.

"Where you came from?" Emma asked. "You mean...you weren't born on Tar Ebon?"

Her mother smiled indulgently at her. "No, honey. We came from another planet called Earth. Like the Founders, but they came from further in our future."

Emma's head spun. "So you traveled here from another planet? And the Founders did too?"

"Through space *and* time," Uncle Jason clarified. "The Founder's records indicated they came from the distant future, a future we," he gestured to himself, Ashley, John, Bridgette and Dawyn, "had not yet lived in yet."

"Did you come by choice?" she asked.

"Nope," her father said. "One second we're in the cafeteria at the local community college, the next we're in a pitch-black cave up in the White Mountains somewhere. The rest is history."

"That's pretty rude," Ethan said. "To not even ask before sending you here."

Their father shrugged. "We never saw who did it, but when we find them, I'm sure your mother will want to give him or her an earful."

Their mother rolled her eyes. "Anyway, we're centuries away from a space program and this keeps the Halls safe for at least that long. We can deal with it again when that time comes."

"If we're still alive by then," their father said. "I mean, sure, we have immortality, but," he mimed his throat being cut and made the appropriately dramatic sound, "we could be dead."

"Let's not talk like that," their mother said.

"All in favor or sending the Halls into orbit," Dawyn prompted, "say 'aye.'"

"Aye," Emma said, followed by everyone but Aunt Bridgette, who stood with arms crossed and a gloomy expression on her face. Isabelle, who had been uncharacteristically quiet, looked to her mother with a worried expression on her face before slowly lifting her hand and speaking the words of affirmation. Feodora followed suit.

"The 'aye's' have it," Dawyn said, then chuckled. "I've always wanted to say that."

"Join the senate, then," Aunt Bridgette grumbled.

"What's the procedure, Jason?" Dawyn asked, ignoring his sister's remark.

"First, we evacuate everyone from the Halls. We have no reliable way to leave the station once it is in orbit, so anyone left behind will be stranded and die in short order. Then, I will ask Bridgette or Isabelle to trigger the deployment procedure, it's quite simple, really, and shift down to the surface behind all of us."

"I'll do it," Isabelle said, speaking for the first time since the dark portal had been closed. "I'll trigger the deployment and shift down to the surface."

"Are you sure?" Uncle Jason asked. "I'm sure your mother would be more than capable."

"She might use the weapons on the Empire first," John said, then chuckled.

Aunt Bridgette glared at her brother-in-law but didn't deny the joking allegation. "I have full confidence in Isabelle's ability to return to the surface before the Halls are anywhere close to orbit."

"It's settled then," Uncle Jason said, seemingly oblivious to the underlying tension in the room, "Isabelle will trigger the deployment and shift down to the ground-based gate."

"And the gateway will cease to work?" their mother asked.

"Yes, the gate seems to have been calibrated based upon the geo-location of the Halls atop this mountain. Any significant adjustment in the altitude, longitude or latitude of the station will break the calibration of the gateway, which is also why I cannot trigger the deployment and run to the gate - there's a good chance the connection would be broken before I reached pedestal."

Emma's father clapped. "Let's get this party started, then!"

"It's an evacuation, not a party," their mother said.

"We can have a party on the ground," their father said, undeterred.

"We can have a big celebration when we get back to Tar Ebon," Dawyn said, mollifying their father. "Defeating Valdorf is something to celebrate."

The decisions made, the group mustered the remaining soldiers and made their way to the gateway console.

Emma stood at the glass panel in the gateway room as the ragged forces of Tar Ebon gathered. She looked south where, through gaps in the clouds, she saw the ocean and, almost at the edge of her vision, the dark clouds heralding the storm wall.

Her father walked up beside her and put a hand on her shoulder. "Whatcha thinking, kid?"

She pointed. "The storm wall. Do you think it'll ever come down?"

"Eh, maybe one day, though I don't know that bringing it down would actually be a good thing."

"Why not?"

He shrugged. "The Founders placed it there for a reason. Your uncle thinks it was in case the Krai'kesh defeated us - the other half of the world could survive - but we don't know what's down there. For all we know, the Krai'kesh could have been down there too and destroyed them already."

"Favio was setting out," Emma began, "he said he was going to go through the storm wall, to see what's on the other side. Do you think he'll make it?"

"Kid, if I could see the future, I'd be rich. But I do know Favio is a hardy man and if the Krai'kesh didn't kill him, I don't think a gigantic storm will." Her father turned her around and looked her in the eyes. "Hey, are you okay?"

Emma sighed. They hadn't had much time to actually *talk* since the revelation that her parents were Eternals. Something which should have been a live-changing event had been overshadowed by the final battle for the survival of the planet. Now that she reflected on it. "You lied to us," she said at last.

He didn't look away, just nodded. "Yeah, we did. Do you know why?"

It was Emma's turn to shrug.

"To protect you."

"From the cultists?"

"Them, and from the effects of fame."

"What do you mean?"

"Well, if you knew you were the children of two of *the* most famous people this side of the ocean it might have changed your view of life. At least that's what your mother and I worried about."

Emma furrowed her brows. "Changed our view how?"

"Back where we came from, kids who were born to famous people, which usually included a lot of wealth, often turned into spoiled brats."

"We knew spoiled brats back in Ironforge," Emma pointed out. "Their parents weren't rich."

"No, spoiled brats aren't exclusive to the rich, but there's a higher percentage of spoiled brats born to wealthy families, at least according to your mother. So we decided it was best to raise you without you knowing who we truly were."

"It kind of back-fired, didn't it? I mean, if you'd been back in Tar Ebon you could have helped against the return of the cultists, could have stopped me and Ethan from almost killing each other, could have…," she stopped, realizing her cheeks were heating as her temper rose. "…Saved my friends."

Her father had the aplomb to look ashamed for moment, breaking eye contact at last. "Life is full of regrets, Emma. But if we live our lives asking 'what if' at every turn, we'll never truly live."

"So you're saying I should just forget about them?" her temper continued to rise. Without her, Kylie would have been alive right now. Probably still in a coven of witches, yes, but alive. *I don't know for sure that she's dead. She was flung through the portal, yes, but so was Valdorf in the last moments of his life and he too could be alive. If they'd wanted her dead wouldn't they have left her here?*

"No. Never forget. But honor their memory by moving forward with your life. Learn from mistakes and accept your regrets as being unchangeable now."

"Will I be immortal, or as good as, like you and Mom and the others?"

"Does that scare you?" his eyes held compassion, as they had many times during her seventeen years of life.

"Yes," she said, admitting out loud what she'd been internalizing since the group conversation earlier. "How do I deal with the friends who will die? I mean, I'm seventeen! I can't even imagine being thirty, let alone three hundred or three thousand!" She'd befriended Princess Feodora over the past several weeks and shuddered at the thought of seeing her friend wither and die one day. *I wish I could see Kylie grow old and die.*

Her father chuckled. "Join the club. I'm what, forty this year, and I don't look a day over twenty if I don't mask my appearance. So technically I haven't reached 'old age' yet. Come back and ask me in fifty years when I've been alive ninety years."

"By then I'll be seventy-three," Emma said dryly.

"You'll be eligible for social security," he said with a smirk.

"What's that?"

"Never mind," he said. "Earth joke."

"Gather 'round, everyone," her mother called, waving her arms.

"I guess we better join the rest," her father said.

"Yeah," Emma agreed, walking toward where dozens of soldiers and her family and friends had gathered. She avoided looking at the unmoving bodies of the dead - they would be given proper burials once they reached the ground. As for the cultists and krai'kesh, smoke drifting from an outer platform marked the location of the pyre burning their bodies. She considered helping the flames out, to burn faster, but her head pounded from channeling so much magic and she wasn't sure she could light a candle.

She strode up to Feodora. "Feodora? Are you all right?"

Feodora, who had been staring at the bodies of the dead soldiers ready to be picked up and carried by their living brethren, turned to Emma. She seemed older, more haunted. But she offered a smile for Emma. "I'm happy to be alive. But the cost...so many dead at the hands of the cultists."

"At least it's over," Emma said. "It could have been much, much worse." *Like apocalypse-level worse.*

"You're right. I'll be glad to get back to my mother and siblings and return to the palace. But I'm sure we'll see each other again, Eternal," she offered a mock curtsy.

Emma flushed. "Hush. I don't like that name." *Nor do I want to admit I'll one day watch you die, princess.*

The princess threw her arms wide. "Then how about I continue calling you Emma, and we hug?"

Emma smiled and embraced her friend. "I would like that." They separated and Feodora went to join a group of soldiers waiting in line.

Ethan stood talking with Dawyn and seemed reluctant to join the group, but did so as Dawyn went to speak to some of the soldiers. He and Richard stood together surveying the scene.

Emma approached him and poked him in the back of the shoulder. "Hey."

He jumped. "Oh, hey, Emma."

"What were you talking to Dawyn about?"

"He wants to be a Ranger," Richard chimed in.

"Hey, I told you that in competence!"

"It's confidence," Emma and Richard said in unison.

"Whatever. I didn't want you to go blurting it to the first person who asked."

"I thought you wanted to be a mage-guard," Emma prompted. "What changed?"

"Well...I can be both. Dawyn said sometimes mages will train as a mage-guard and then come to the Rangers. And given my newfound status..."

"Which Dawyn has technically known about since the first time he set eyes upon us," Emma put in dourly. *Were we the worst-kept secret on the continent?*

"...I can be an officer right after training," Ethan finished.

"You, an officer?" Emma asked, rolling her eyes. "Founders help those poor soldiers," she jested.

"Shut up. I have to finish my mage-guard training first. I'll be more mature."

Emma stifled a laugh and sought to change the subject. "What about you, Richard?"

"Maybe I'll serve General Ethan one day," he joked. "I'm with him, though. We're going to do our mage-guard training and go from there. You?"

Emma snorted. "Slayer of evil god-worshiping evil-doers? No, I'll probably go down and see Frederik. Maybe Isabelle can give me a ride on her parent's boat."

"Giving up on mage-guard training so soon?" Ethan asked.

"It's still summer vacation. For a few more weeks, anyway," she said dully.

"Gateway is opening!" her mother called. "Single file!"

"Yes, Mother," Ethan grumbled. "What if we all just ran through at once? Would she yell at us?"

"You're never too old to get your ass swatted," Emma said. Her eyes fell on Isabelle, who watched from the doorway. It was her job to activate the orbital protocol once the last person went through. She walked over to her.

Isabelle smiled nervously as Emma approached. "Hey."

"Hey yourself," Emma said. "Cousin." It felt surreal to call her that. In the heat of the moment they hadn't had time to pause and reflect on the revelations that day. "You nervous about doing this?"

"You mean about having to shift from way up here down to the ground before the Halls reach orbit and I'm stuck up there? No, not a bit." The sarcasm dripped from her last sentence.

"Maybe one day you and your mom will learn how to shift in outer space. Who knows, maybe you'll be able to travel to the moon or something using your powers."

Isabelle rolled her eyes. "I seriously doubt that." She pointed. "The line is shrinking."

"I know. Hey, when this is over, do you think we could go visit Frederik?"

She raised an eyebrow. "What, need to get some kissing in before the next semester? I'm sure Richard would oblige."

"Shut up!" Emma said, punching her cousin in the shoulder and feeling her cheeks warm. "Richard doesn't like me like that."

"Really? Could have fooled me."

Emma looked behind her to where Richard and Ethan stood in line near the back. He *was* handsome, in a rugged way. But Frederik had that regal composure she found attractive. And, before she'd learned of her true lineage, the influence and money that could have helped her family. What would he think of her when he learned the truth? She pushed that, and any romantic thoughts Richard might have of her, out of her mind. Those were problems for another time.

She turned back to Isabelle and smiled. "Good luck."

"I'll need it," she said with a smirk.

Emma ran to join her brother and, with her mother and father behind her, stepped through the gate.

EMMA STOOD IN THE COURTYARD of Landgren keep as the last of the soldiers came through with a wagon piled with corpses. She refused to look away as they passed. *We must honor the dead.*

The portal wavered and winked out. Emma suppressed the urge to feel panic, for she knew this was expected. She exchanged glances with her brother, who nodded reassuringly. Behind him, Richard offered a small smile before averting his eyes. *Insufferable boy,* Emma thought.

The princess had already ridden back to reunite with her family, while her parents had gone off with Jason and Dawyn to discuss their strategy against the remaining cultists. Only her Aunt Bridgette remained with Ethan, Richard and Emma. She stalked back and forth behind the portal, wearing a path in the grass there.

Moments passed into minutes and ten minutes had passed before shadowy mist coalesced into Isabelle.

Emma let out a "whoop" and started clapping, glad to see her friend and cousin returned safe. She ran to embrace her, joined by her Aunt Bridgette, while Ethan and Richard ran out of the courtyard to bring the good news to the others.

They had lost many friends and allies, but they'd saved the world. That had to count for something, right? As Emma looked skyward, she remembered the words of the seraphim. "Prepare." *Will we be ready?*

The End

Don't miss out!

Visit the website below and you can sign up to receive emails whenever Dayne Edmondson publishes a new book. There's no charge and no obligation.

https://books2read.com/r/B-A-ZEND-KQTS

BOOKS 2 READ

Connecting independent readers to independent writers.

Did you love *Halls of Light*? Then you should read *Ghost Ranger* by Dayne Edmondson!

My name is Rachel. I **died and rose again**.

I was an ordinary high school girl when a viral plague spread across my planet. Those that died rose again as mindless zombies. Fortunately, science came to the rescue and gave me back my mind. As a conscious zombie, I gained exceptional powers – speed, strength and more. That, plus a secret heritage, changed my life forever.

The outside world didn't accept my kind, however, and soon I decided to join the military. I trained to become an Army Ranger.

Now, as an elite undead killing machine, I must make a choice. Allegiance to my kind or to the Federation. Choose wrong and I could die...for good.

Another installment in the Seven Stars Universe by Dayne Edmondson, this is a young adult space opera adventure novel set a few years before his space opera novel "Emergence" and featuring a major character from the third book, "Ruin."

Buy now to jump into the adventure.

Read more at https://www.darkstarpublishing.com.

Also by Dayne Edmondson

The Dark Tide Trilogy
Emergence
Eclipse
Ruin

The Mageborn Saga
Mageborn
The Cursed Tower
Halls of Light

The Seven Stars Universe
Ghost Ranger
Space Commando

The Shadow Trilogy
Blood and Shadows
Time of Shadows
Shadows Fall

Standalone
The Complete Dark Tide Trilogy
The Complete Shadow Trilogy

Watch for more at https://www.darkstarpublishing.com.

About the Author

Dayne Edmondson lives in southeastern Michigan with his wife and two young children, a boy and a girl. He writes part time and works a day job.

His books can be read in this order:

<u>The Shadow Trilogy</u>:
1. Blood and Shadows
2. Time of Shadows
3. Shadows Fall

<u>Mageborn Saga:</u>
1. Mageborn
2. The Cursed Tower
3. Halls of Light (coming 2019)

<u>The Seven Stars Universe</u>:
1. Ghost Ranger (coming 2019)

<u>The Dark Tide Trilogy:</u>
1. Emergence
2. Eclipse
3. Ruin

Dayne enjoys reading, writing, the occasional video game, watching TV with his wife, walking and spending time with his children indoors or out.

He writes and reads science fiction and fantasy. Some of his favorite authors/books include Robert Jordan, Brandon Sanderson, (almost) all the Star Wars EU books, Elizabeth Haydon, Christopher Nuttall and more.

Read more at https://www.darkstarpublishing.com.

About the Publisher

Dark Star Publishing is a small-press publisher of science fiction and fantasy novels. They place particular emphasis on books written **in** the Seven Stars Universe (the universe created by author and owner Dayne Edmondson).

For more information, visit https://www.darkstarpublishing.com